CATCHING HELL

by GREG F. GIFUNE

With Billy in the lead, the quartet left the car on the outskirts of Main Street and walked toward the center of town. The park and gazebo on the first block were empty. The post office that followed was closed, and the police station next door sat vacant.

As they ventured farther, marching right up the middle of the street, they saw that the general store had also been shut down.

Everything was abandoned. What few townspeople had been there previously had seemingly locked up and walked away.

"When's the last time you saw a police station close?" Billy asked. The heels of his scuffed boots clacked pavement, and as he keyed on the cadence, something else occurred to him. He came to a stop. The others did the same. "Listen. There aren't even any birds singing. None in the sky, either."

"I haven't seen an animal since we got here," Alex said. "Not even a bug."

"Are you guys sure getting out of the car is a good idea?" Tory asked.

Dedication

For Sandy DeLuca.

And for J R, who was there.

Thanks to my friends, fans and readers. Also, thanks to my colleague and buddy, film director/writer Jay Woelfel, for the helpful discussions we had regarding this project when it was still in the conceptual stage. Thanks to Rob Dunbar for the afternoon chats that made me laugh and kept me (relatively) sane. Thanks to Rich Chizmar and Cemetery Dance Publications for first publishing CATCHING HELL and getting it out to the world back in 2010. And special thanks to David Wilson and everyone at Crossroad Press/Macabre Ink for releasing CATCHING HELL back out to the masses in this new paperback edition.

AN UPDATED AUTHOR'S NOTE

Catching Hell, first published in 2010, was inspired by incidents I experienced in the early 1980s. As the Phaedrus quote states: "Things are not always as they seem." If life has taught me anything, it is that. Although I am no closer now to understanding what took place than I was the day it happened, I can tell you that those events have stayed with me, and the other person primarily involved, and continue to haunt us even more than three decades later. I suspect they always will. It is my hope that you'll never know anything similar in your life, but I do hope this bit of fiction will stay with you in much the same, albeit safer and hopefully entertaining way. Just remember to watch yourself out there. Sometimes the road is treacherous, and things are most certainly not always as they seem. Not then. Not now.

—Greg F. Gifune
Monday, September 30th, 2019
New England. Night.

INSPIRED BY TRUE EVENTS

"The first condition of immortality is death."

—*Stanislaw J. Lec*

Chapter One

Something had prevented her from dreaming. Normally a light sleeper, she often found herself lying awake in the night, momentarily stunned and unsure of where she was. But her sleep had been unusually deep this time, and she awakened with a quiet sense of purpose, which like the coming dawn grew steadily stronger.

A breeze brought wind chimes outside the bedroom window to life, their delicate, otherworldly music drifting through the mostly dark room. A lovely sound, she thought, but strangely melancholy as well.

The shadows parted as she sat up, and the beginnings of daylight bled through the windows, gently absorbing the darkness, devouring it slowly. She had a strong desire to stand before the mirror against the far wall, to look at her reflection, to see firsthand what had become of her during such a long and unforgiving night. But she remained in bed, remembering.

They were all so impossibly young that summer of '83. She'd still been a teenager, for God's sake. Such a very long time ago.

Yet it seemed like only yesterday.

She touched her face, searched it for wrinkles.

2001. *My God*, she thought, *I'm thirty-seven years old. All those years, all that precious time, come and gone.*

She reached for the man next to her and touched his shoulder, as if to be certain he was more than a remnant of night, a residual phantom; hypnotic spots left in the wake of a photographer's flash.

"I'm here," he said groggily.

And she remembered then what had awakened her. "You were crying."

He turned his head, sad eyes blinking through fading darkness.

"Just now," she told him, "in your sleep. You were weeping."

With a sigh, he looked away, joining her if only for a moment in the deliverance of the past.

1983 was a violent year. On February 24th, at the age of 72, legendary playwright Tennessee Williams died of asphyxiation when a bottle cap became lodged in his throat and blocked his airway. The drugs and alcohol he had ingested left him unable to call for help, and he died alone, lending added poignancy to one of his more prophetic sayings: "Whether or not we admit it to ourselves, we are all haunted by a truly awful sense of impermanence." Later that same year, on April 28, the government of Argentina announced that all 30,000 persons who had gone missing in their country during the military dictatorship that began in 1976 were dead. On August 30th, a South Korean commercial jetliner was shot down by a Soviet SU-15 fighter after it mistakenly strayed into Russian airspace. All 269 people aboard were killed. On October 23rd, a terrorist bomb killed 237 U.S. Marines in Beirut, and two days later the United States invaded Grenada. In the U.S. alone, more than 150,000 people simply vanished, the overwhelming majority children, and all but a small percentage twenty-one or younger. Few were ever found or heard from again, and most were assumed to have met violent ends.

That summer of '83 had been particularly violent for Billy Valerio and the others too, but in a very different way. Ironically, it felt infinitely more real than those horrible things happening in other places to other people, but they had no way of knowing then what was waiting for them in those waning days of summer.

From his cushioned seat, Billy came awake, drifting from the murky darkness of sleep until the apartment before him came into view. He paid particular attention to the short staircase just inside the front door. He'd killed from the top of those stairs for the last several weeks, stabbing Stefan in the back then watching as his body toppled and rolled to the bottom step in a heap. From there, he'd spent night after night terrorizing poor Alex and chasing her around the small apartment before himself being killed in her last-ditch effort to save herself.

But he'd done more here over the last seven summers than assume the role of psychopath Harry Roat in the thriller *Wait Until Dark*. Years before, at just fourteen, he'd debuted as a suicidal mental patient in *One Flew Over the Cuckoo's Nest*, and then gone on to play a bevy of diverse roles that had helped him hone his craft as an actor and prepare him for what was still to come, the next step in his career: a move to New York City. The big-time, the real thing, and a journey he'd dreamed of since he was a child. Now, at twenty-one, he found himself staring at a stage in one of the older and more successful summer stock theaters on Cape Cod. He'd spent hours performing, rehearsing, learning and evolving on that stage, but the night before had been his final appearance, his time here was done. Within hours a crew was scheduled to tear down the set and close the theater until the following season.

But this wasn't only Billy's final season here; it was Stefan and Alex's too. Stefan, who joined the troupe two years after Billy did, had been his best friend since both were sixteen, and though, with the exception of this last production, he hadn't landed many of the choice roles Billy had, he'd always been more focused on his writing anyway and hoped to one day fulfill his dream of becoming a successful playwright. Alexis Flynn was a few years younger than both of them, and rather than working the majority of her teenage years as an actor, had only signed with the theater two years prior, at seventeen, just after graduating high school. For the past year they'd all shared an apartment down by the ocean together, and in her time at the theater she'd been briefly romantically involved with Billy and Stefan both. It soon became evident, however, that they'd make better friends than lovers, and the three settled into a close friendship instead.

Since her arrival, Alex had also skyrocketed to leading roles, including her latest as Suzy in *Wait Until Dark*, a performance that had brought the house down nightly for the last several weeks. She'd recently received a scholarship to attend the acting program at Emerson College in Boston, and planned to leave for school in the coming weeks while Billy and Stefan were set to load what little they had into Stefan's old Ford Fairlane and head to Manhattan to chase their dreams.

But first they'd planned a vacation getaway to Maine for a few days. Alex's uncle managed a summer resort not far from Bar Harbor, and since tourist season was essentially over there too, he'd invited his niece and her friends to visit and use the facilities free of charge for a weekend. They all knew it might be the last time they were together again, so it was a bittersweet proposition, but also one they couldn't pass up. Spending their final weekend together basking beneath the last of the summer sunshine at a beautiful resort was, if nothing else, a fitting last hoorah for the trio, a long weekend of fun and relaxation before real life again came knocking.

The night before, at the conclusion of the final show, the cast and crew celebrated with a huge end-of-season party, and somewhere along the line Billy had lost track of everyone else and ended up back at the theater.

As he sat up, a sharp pain shot from the back of his neck into his skull. He grabbed his cigarettes and a Zippo from the seat to his left then pulled his legs from the back of the chair in front of him. His hamstrings and lower back tensed, reminding him what a terrible idea it had been to sleep in such a position, and suddenly the concept of spending the next several hours in a car trekking to Maine seemed anything but appealing.

Pushing a cigarette into the corner of his mouth, Billy sparked the lighter, inhaled then coughed out a cloud of smoke. Hair mussed and in need of a shave, it wasn't until he absently scratched at his stomach that he realized he was nude.

"You're awake." Dressed only in a pair of bikini panties, a young woman with shoulder-length bleached hair sauntered in from a small hallway to the right of the stage.

"Somewhat," he said, voice raspy. "Um…line?"

"Jesse."

"Jesse. Right. Cool."

"Nice of you to remember." She found her bra draped over the back of a nearby seat and wiggled her breasts into it. After fastening it, she stepped into her uniform, a bright polyester dress. "I figured it'd be okay to use the bathroom in that office."

"There any aspirin back there?"

"I don't know. You're the one who works here."

On the seat next to him, not far from where his cigarettes and lighter had been, Billy saw what was left of a bottle of Jack Daniel's. He scooped it up, spun the cap and threw some back. "Not anymore."

"Gross, you're drinking? You can't drink this time of day."

Through bleary eyes, he considered the bottle. "Apparently I can."

"It's not even nine o'clock in the morning. You shouldn't party so hard."

"Didn't we just meet last night?"

"So? Look at you, you're a mess."

Billy located his clothes in a pile next to a rumpled blanket on the floor in front of the stage. As he inched his way down the row of seats, he said, "OK, let's review." He left the cigarette between his lips, moved to the blanket and stepped into an old pair of Levis. "You work as a waitress at a fried clam shack in a Cape Cod resort town, you fuck loser small-time actors like me from the local repertory theater because—let's face it—we may not be anything special but at least we're a step up from the lowlife redneck townies you usually spend your Saturday nights blowing. Your favorite TV show is *The Love Boat* and the last book you read had pop-ups in it. Sound about right?"

"You're an asshole."

"Hey, it's a skill like any other."

"I was just trying to help you." She slung a large purse over her shoulder, straightened her hair then headed for the exit. "Whatever, I'm history."

"Wait," he said, head bowed. "I didn't...I didn't mean any of that, OK?"

"Sure you did." Her eyes remained cold. "But you know what? You're no different than I am. We've got the same life waiting for us. The only difference is I know it."

She rammed the exit door with her shoulder and stormed out.

A swath of sunshine flooded the theater in her wake, catching the small dagger earring dangling from Billy's left lobe. With a sigh, he collapsed into a seat in the front row. "Jesus."

"Like He'd help *your* lame ass."

Alex. Standing in the open doorway, she leaned against the frame, pushed out her bottom lip and blew a renegade strand of hair from her forehead. Just over five feet barefoot, she was petite and at first glance could easily be mistaken for a child. But closer inspection revealed she was entirely woman. She'd styled her hair into a short pixie-cut for the part of Suzy (in tribute to Audrey Hepburn's portrayal in the film), and dyed it from its natural chestnut to black. With a little styling mousse, she'd given it a new wave look, and though she rarely wore much makeup, the black liner she'd applied earlier helped accentuate her large brown eyes.

"Just keeping the faith, baby."

"Somebody better." She bent down and grabbed Billy's boots and T-shirt. "Figured I'd find you here."

"It's not the first night I've slept in the seats." He took a swallow of JD. "But I guess it'll be the last, huh?"

Alex threw the boots at his feet and snatched the bottle away. "Give me that, you idiot. What the hell's wrong with you?"

"Best thing in the world for a hangover."

She fired the T-shirt at him. It landed draped across his head. "Come on, get dressed, we've got a long ride ahead of us and Stef's waiting." She put the bottle on the edge of the stage then looked around in a slow pirouette. "God, I'm going to miss this place."

"Lots of memories."

"Part of me wishes we were all coming back for another season."

"Can't stay in the minor leagues forever."

She gave a sad nod.

Billy watched her a moment. In a loose-fitting Pat Benatar concert sweatshirt that hung low on one shoulder, black jeans and a pair of white sneakers, he was certain she'd never looked at once sexier or more vibrant. She seemed on the brink of something better, an eventual greatness few would ever have the chance to experience.

He maneuvered into his boots. "I haven't even packed yet."

"I already packed your things into that disgusting duffel of yours."

He forced himself to his feet with a grunt. "What about the rent?"

"Stef and I took care of it. You can square up with us later."

"Thanks."

"Did you really think we expected you to be together and ready on time?"

He squinted at the open doorway. "Listen, can you help me find my—"

"Sure." A pair of black wayfarer sunglasses seemed to magically appear in Alex's hand. "No problem."

"What would I do without you?"

"You'd survive. You're Billy the Kid." She winked at him playfully, the way she often did. "You can do anything."

With a devilish grin, Billy slid the sunglasses on. "Then let's go to Maine."

At six-two and weighing no more than one hundred and fifty pounds, Stefan Boudreau was tall and lean to the point of sometimes looking emaciated. But he carried himself with a natural grace and style, his movement conservative yet fluid, his behavior reserved but not quite aloof, and his mind blessed with a quick, often stinging wit. His pensive eyes and angular features resulted in a look somewhere between a young David Bowie and an even younger Donald Sutherland, and though he was only twenty-one and known for his sense of humor and the ability to somehow keep pace with Billy's crazed drinking, in many ways Stefan seemed an old soul.

Leaned against the front grill of his somewhat dilapidated but dependable '67 Ford Fairlane, arms folded across his chest and sporting an ironic smile, Stefan watched Alex and Billy's approach. Dark sunglasses shielded his eyes, and he was clad in a pair of khaki shorts, maroon penny loafers and a yellow Izod shirt. His wispy brown hair—normally worn to his collar but cut and styled more conservatively for his role as Mike Talman in *Wait Until Dark*—was combed neatly into place and still wet from a recent shower.

"Hey, look," Billy said as he drew nearer. "It's Thurston Howell the third."

"Style, laundry detergent and ironing," Stefan replied without altering his expression. "Look into them, won't you?"

"Oh, dah-ling," Alex said in her most theatrical voice, "I think you look positively dashing!"

Stefan replied in kind. "Oh, thank you dah-ling!"

"No, no, thank *you* dah-ling!"

Billy sighed wearily. "How long is this fucking ride again?"

"Six, seven hours," Alex beamed.

"Just kill me now. Run me over with the car."

Alex put an arm around both men and pulled them close to her. As one, they turned and looked back at the theater, sitting in the middle of a dirt parking lot at the end of a nondescript country road. No one spoke for a very long time.

"Hey, guys!"

From the field behind them came Tory Gruden, a twenty-year-old stagehand they'd only known a few months but had befriended during the season. With his long blond hair, blue eyes, vacuous good looks and deep tan, he looked like a surfer from central casting. As he bounded across the field, one hand holding a straw cowboy hat in place and the other toting a small suitcase, he smiled and called out to them again. "Sorry I'm late!"

"What the hell's he doing here?" Billy asked.

Alex gave a timid smile. "He asked if he could come."

"Yeah, seriously, you know what? Run me over."

"Stop, he'll hear you." She elbowed him. "Stefan didn't mind and I didn't think you would either. I felt bad for him. He's like an abandoned puppy, he's—"

"He's Jeff Spicoli."

"He had nowhere to go and we're his only friends and—"

"OK, OK, whatever. If nothing else, he's always got good weed on him."

Tory stumbled into the lot, the seashells on his necklace clacking together. "Tasty rays today!" In cutoff shorts, flip-flops and a tie-dye T-shirt, he already looked ready for poolside. "I'm stoked, never been to Maine before. I hear it's totally bodacious."

"Great." Billy headed for the passenger seat. "You're like a living caricature, only worse. Try not to talk again until we get there, OK?"

Tory frowned. "Whoa, mucho negativity energy alert, man."

"He's kidding." Alex guided him toward the trunk so he could stow away his things. "He has a headache."

"Hey, no problem-o, bro, I got some doobage that'll fix that right up."

"On that note," Stefan said, grinning, "let's ramble."

The sky was a perfect crystal blue, void of clouds, and though the sun burned high and bright, humidity was low, so despite the rather tight quarters the car remained comfortable.

Billy drifted off to sleep even before they'd reached the Bourne Bridge, one of two enormous structures that connected Cape Cod to the mainland. The last thing he saw was trees and brush along the side of the Cape Cod highway rushing past his window.

"Some copilot," Stefan quipped. "He's supposed to be riding shotgun."

"We should be to Boston in about an hour," Alex said, "then figure another two to Portland, give or take. Once we get somewhere between the two, stop for a bathroom break and I'll switch with him, OK?" She leaned forward to check on Billy. "Have you ever seen anyone sleep the way he does?"

"Not outside a mortuary."

When they'd been a couple, Alex remembered watching him sleep on more than one occasion, and how his face often looked tormented or frightened even when he was deeply asleep. This time was no exception.

"Wish I could sleep better," Tory said, injecting himself into their conversation. "I can get to sleep, but I never *stay* asleep, you know? I wake up like every hour or so. It totally blows chimps."

Stefan caught Alex's eyes in the rearview and fired off his

best wiseass smirk. "All that critical thinking must be keeping you up."

"Huh?"

"He just means you seem so mellow," Alex said, trying not to laugh.

"I am pretty laid back." Tory looked out the window with an unusually pensive expression. "But we all got demons."

Surprised by the response, Stefan returned his attention to the road.

Alex sat back without comment. Beside her, Tory placed the hat over his face and folded his arms across his chest.

But for the steady hum of wind through the open windows, silence fell over the car. Alex again sat forward, this time saying nothing.

"Are you all right?" Stefan asked.

"I don't know, little scared about school."

"It'll be great. Think of the things you'll learn. Besides, you'll have two years of legitimate stage experience up on everyone else. You'll be amazing."

Alex smiled. She could always count on Stefan to say things like that, and whenever he did, it reminded her of what a gentle, giving and sweetly awkward lover he had been. "Maybe I should just go to New York with you guys."

"Look, this is a big chance for you. Emerson's program is outstanding. You're getting an opportunity a lot of us never will, Alex, remember that."

She had listened before to Stefan recount how his parents considered his dream of being a playwright and actor foolishness, and how they had insisted he take something practical so he could earn a decent living. She also knew Billy had come from a relatively supportive family but had struggled in high school with a severe authority problem, and had been thrown out of several schools, which labeled him a troubled case and ruined his chances at college. "At least Billy's got lots of professional experience and you have a degree," she reminded him.

"An Associate's in Accounting," he said. "Can you imagine anything more mundane? I'd rather put a gun in my mouth than ever put it to use."

"You could get a real job if need be. What the hell am I going to do with a degree in theater arts, whip it out at my auditions? But wait, I have a degree!"

"If all else fails, you can wind up an aging, bitter, alcoholic drama teacher at some high school somewhere, directing hideous productions of *Arsenic and Old Lace* and *West Side Story* year after year."

"Don't forget *Oklahoma!*"

"God knows I've tried."

"Don't worry. I'll hire you every tax season."

They let the sounds of the road take over a second time. "Seriously," Stefan eventually said, "you'll do fine, don't give it another thought. And once you've graduated, we'll be waiting. Literally. We'll be waiting tables. But still."

Alex laughed, though the same nagging nervousness she'd felt for days continued to gnaw at her. "What'll I do without you guys?"

"Come on, I just spent the summer conning you then getting stabbed in the back and falling down a staircase four nights a week—twice on Saturdays—and you've spent it being terrorized by Billy's Mr. Roat. I'd think you'd be sick of us by now." He reached back and touched her hand with his own. "Alex, you've got more talent than Billy and I do put together. You're the one who's got a real chance at making it, and those four years at Emerson will only make you better. It's the smart move. Make it."

She leaned in and kissed his cheek. "I love you."

"Of course you do," he said, returning his hand to the wheel. "It's called taste, darling." And then, after a moment, softly, "I love you too. Now sit back and leave me alone before I wretch."

As the huge arched top of the Bourne Bridge appeared at the edge of the horizon, Stefan switched on the radio and turned the dial until he'd found a Top 40 station. With A Flock of Seagulls blaring through the speakers, he pressed harder on the gas and sped toward the bridge, leaving Cape Cod behind them.

Chapter Two

By the time they'd made it through Boston and merged onto I-95 toward New Hampshire, Billy had come awake. "Are we there yet, Mommy?"

Stefan waved thanks to another motorist for letting him change lanes. "Not even in New Hampshire yet, Scooter."

Mumbling something unintelligible, Billy wrapped his arms around himself, turned toward the door and fell back to sleep.

Tory smiled dreamily. "Thanks again for letting me come, Alex."

"Don't be silly, happy to have you. Got anything going off-season?"

"My old man owns a landscaping company in Jersey, said he could get me work, so I'll probably hitchhike down there."

"Is your mom there too?"

"Nah, she's back home in Rhode Island."

"What does she do?"

"Heroin mostly."

Alex froze. "Jesus, Tory, I—I'm sorry."

"Don't sweat it." He shrugged. "We all got problems. That's hers."

Unsure of what else to do, Alex responded with a solemn nod. She hoped Stefan might rescue her but he was fiddling with the radio, so she put her head back, closed her eyes and concentrated on the motion of the car. She embraced its subtle tempo and realized there was a rhythm to it, like the slow cadence of a heartbeat, or the shallow rise and fall of her chest with each breath drawn then expelled. *Like something alive,* she thought.

Or something slowly dying.

After two hours of small talk, occasional silence, group

sing-alongs with the radio and Billy's perpetual snoring, they had passed through New Hampshire, crossed into Maine and arrived in the city of Portland.

Stefan found a fast-food joint and pulled in so everyone could take a bathroom break and stretch their legs a bit. Since they'd made good time and it was only noon, they settled for coffee or soda and agreed to put off lunch and pull over again later, once they'd been on the road another hour or so.

When they piled back into the Fairlane, Alex took the front passenger seat and Billy joined Tory in back. Within minutes, they had returned to the highway.

As they continued toward Bangor, north along I-95, they left any semblance of city life in the rearview and ventured into a far wilder and more rustic landscape. On occasion, they passed a residence set back in the heavily wooded area through which the highway cut its path—sometimes a home built up into the side of a distant hill or nestled amidst the forest, sometimes a trailer standing alone, tires on the roof and a rusted pickup parked alongside it—but for the most part the route, though at times wonderfully scenic, was fairly standard highway fair. Traffic was also far lighter than it had been in Massachusetts and New Hampshire, and the farther they went, the fewer cars they saw.

Throughout, the weather remained sunny and beautiful, the sky clear and bright, which is why they were taken so completely by surprise when seemingly out of nowhere a bank of thick dark clouds suddenly appeared on the horizon.

"Wow," Stefan muttered. "Look at that."

Alex, who had been reclining in the passenger seat, one foot on the dash and the other out the window and supported by the side mirror, sat up and pulled her foot back inside. "Where did those come from?"

"Roll the windows up. It's running right into us." Stefan removed his sunglasses, hung them on the front of his shirt and quickly closed his window.

As they collided with the storm, the sky turned black, day turned to night, and a violent downpour assaulted the car.

Rain poured across the windshield in a thick and steady

stream, and even with the wipers on full tilt, the watery veil made visibility all but impossible. The radio station they'd been listening to faded in and out, losing strength the farther they drove until it finally fell silent.

Alex shifted her gaze from window to window. "This is way too dangerous to be driving in."

"Yeah, I'm pulling over," Stefan agreed. "I can't see a damn thing."

In the back seat, Tory was asleep and hadn't stirred. Next to him, Billy's nose was buried in a dog-eared paperback edition of Stanislavski's classic, *An Actor Prepares*. "What happened to the tunes?" he asked absently. "I believe the brochure for this tour promised continuous tunes."

"I've never seen anything like this," Stefan said, clutching the wheel with a white-knuckled grip and easing the car to the side of the road. "It came out of nowhere."

The sudden darkness forced Billy to glance up from his book. "Holy shit."

Rain drummed the roof with such ferocity it was deafening, and Tory finally came awake. "What's with the waterworks?" he asked through a yawn.

As the car rolled to a stop, Stefan dropped the shift into park and sat back, relieved. "We ran into a little unexpected storm."

"Cool." Tory pulled a joint from his side pocket. "Let's get lightly toasted."

"Do *not* light that in here," Stefan snapped. "If the rain doesn't let up, I'll have to drive in this shit, which should be enough of a bitch without being stoned out of my mind."

Tory slid the joint behind his ear. "Sorry."

"Hey, commander," Billy said with a smirk, "OK with you if I smoke a butt?"

Stefan rubbed his eyes. "You know, I was just thinking this situation needed a little more sarcasm."

Billy lit a cigarette. "I do what I can."

The rain stopped. Suddenly, as it had begun.

Water sluiced along the windows and windshield, parted by the wipers to reveal sunshine. "OK," Alex said, "I'm glad that wasn't too weird."

Stefan looked to the sky. The blue, cloudless canopy had returned in all its grandeur. "Must've just been a freak downpour."

"No harm no foul." Billy exhaled a stream of smoke at the back of his head and slid his wayfarers on. "Let's hit it, Magellan."

As Stefan reached for the shift, a moving blur appeared just beyond the windshield, a black smudge hurtling toward them that swooped down so fast they didn't have time to process it or react.

The blackbird smashed head-first into the windshield with a loud and sickening thud that shook the entire car.

Alex screamed and Stefan ducked, raising his hands defensively as blood sprayed the windshield and the animal fell away, rolled off the hood and toppled to the pavement. A small hairline crack in the glass appeared, smeared with gore.

"Oh my God!"

"What the hell was that, a bird?"

"Oh my God!"

"Is everybody all right?"

"Did you see that?"

"Jesus, that scared the shit out of me!"

Stefan opened his door and stepped out, nearly falling in his haste, but as he rounded the front of the car, he came to a sudden stop.

The bird was gone. Except for the blood smears on the windshield, there was no trace of it whatsoever.

Stefan crouched and checked beneath the vehicle. Nothing.

"Where is it?" Alex asked, trembling hands to her mouth.

"I don't know, I—There's no way it could've survived that impact." Stefan pointed to the windshield. "Look at the blood."

"Maybe it's just, like, stunned," Tory said, "and—"

"No, that—that bird was dead," Alex insisted, wiping a tear from the corner of her eye. "You heard how hard it hit us. I saw the poor thing's neck break."

Throughout, Billy remained quiet. Positioned in the breakdown lane a few feet from the front of the car, he faced the windshield and smoked his cigarette without comment, eyes masked by sunglasses.

Stefan ran his hands through his hair. "So where the hell is it?"

"This kind of thing happens sometimes."

The others turned to Billy in unison.

"What are you talking about?"

"The old folks in my family, my grandmother and all the ones born back in Italy, used to talk about this kind of thing when I was a kid. It's superstition from the old country. When a bird hits a window then disappears, it's a harbinger."

Alex hugged herself. "Of what?"

Billy flicked the cigarette away then turned toward the highway. "Death."

There were still no other cars in sight, and but for a gentle breeze that blew through the trees and across the highway, the road was eerily silent.

"You can't honestly believe that nonsense," Stefan scoffed. "Let's all just calm down. Obviously the bird wasn't killed."

"You just got through saying there was no way it could survive the impact," Alex reminded him. "Which is it, Stefan?"

"Well obviously, *Alexis*, the goddamn thing's still alive, isn't it? It has to be. I don't see how but apparently it survived. There's no other explanation. It certainly didn't vanish into thin air. Can we agree on that or have you collectively lost your minds?"

She drew a deep breath and let it out slowly. "Yeah, you—you're right—of course. I bet it got caught in that storm and was disoriented. It must've limped off into the woods or—"

"That's bullshit and you both know it."

"Billy, please." Stefan waved his hand, shooing him away. "A bird flew into the car and startled us. Clearly it was injured but survived. There's nothing else to discuss unless you expect us to believe a bunch of old wives' tales."

"I always thought it was superstition too. But listen to this. When I was twelve, I was sitting in the kitchen with my parents having breakfast one morning, and all of a sudden this blackbird flew right into the window over the sink. It hit so hard it spattered blood all over the pane. Just like this, there was no way it could've lived through it. I went outside with my father to pick up the body and get rid of it. Only there wasn't any body. The bird was gone. We were still looking when my mother called out for us to come back inside because my aunt was on the phone. My grandmother had just died."

"*Radical*," Tory said in a loud, awestruck whisper.

"It's known as a coincidence. They happen all the time." Stefan indicated a road leading off the highway not far from where they'd pulled over. "Is that an exit?"

"There's no sign," Alex said. "Might be a service road, I'm not sure."

"Why don't we get off the highway and go find somewhere to eat?" Stefan moved back toward the car. "We can take a break and recharge our batteries before we make the last push to Bar Harbor. Sound good?"

As Tory climbed into the back seat and Stefan slid behind the wheel, Alex approached Billy and put a hand on his shoulder. She'd never known him to be easily rattled or intimidated. If anything, he often behaved with recklessness that bordered on insanity. "Are you OK?"

Billy looked at her, saying nothing.

"If it makes you feel any better, it spooked me, too." She offered an empathetic smile. "But we can't stand out here all day because a bird hit the windshield. The sooner we get back in the car and on the road, the sooner we can get to the resort and forget about this."

He remained silent.

"*Please*, Billy. Let's just go, all right?"

Finally, he gave a halfhearted nod, and together, they returned to the car.

Chapter Three

Though the road bore no exit sign, by the time they'd gotten to it they could see it wasn't a service road but rather an alternate route from the highway that clearly led somewhere. They followed the winding off-ramp into a heavily wooded area that eventually ended at a stop sign intersected by a single, larger road. Directly across from the sign, a weather-beaten billboard read: Boxer Hills. Pop. 180.

"Boxer Hills," Stefan said. "Never heard of that one before."

"There are lots of tiny towns tucked away up here," Alex said. "The kind of places that generally go unnoticed unless you happen to run into them. They're even more common the farther north you go. Some places don't even have names. They're identified by numbers on maps."

"Enchanting." Stefan rolled his eyes and turned left at the stop sign. "Let's just hope they have a restaurant in this burg."

The country road cut through more thick forest, continuing on for several miles before emptying into what appeared to be the town's main street.

"Civilization!" Alex announced as she sat forward and grabbed the dash.

Stefan removed his sunglasses for a better look. "Hardly."

They drove down the main drag, a remarkably small stretch of road, either side of which was lined with expertly pruned trees. A modest but beautiful park with a sizeable gazebo at its center dominated the first block, followed by an antiquated-looking post office and police station. A weathered general store that resembled something out of a Norman Rockwell painting sat at the end of the street. From its old wooden porch and stairs to its squat, rectangular design, to the bay window segregated into small square panes facing the street, right down to the dirt parking lot, it—like the entire street—could've easily passed for a movie set from the 1940s.

A few additional buildings were sprinkled along another street just beyond the general store, including a quaint Victorian-style library. Next door sat an unassuming firehouse, followed by a dilapidated gas station with a garage and one antique pump. At the end of the street, a windowless stone structure that appeared to be a church of some kind rounded out Boxer Hills's downtown area.

"Great." Stefan sighed. "We're in fucking Mayberry."

"Oh come on," Alex said, laughing, "it's just a little backwoods town, it's adorable."

"Where's the restaurant?" Tory asked.

Stefan pulled into the dirt lot in front of the general store. "I think it's safe to assume we're looking at it. Hopefully they have sandwiches or something. If not, we'll get back on the highway and try the next exit."

"I really need to use a bathroom," Alex said.

"You'd be better off trying the gas station." He pointed farther down the road. "They usually have one."

"I'll go with you," Tory said. "I gotta take a squirt, too."

They all piled out of the car, Billy still conspicuously silent.

"We'll go see if they have anything lunch-like," Stefan said.

"OK, meet you back here in a sec."

Billy watched Alex and Tory cross the street and head for the gas station. They looked as wildly out of place as he felt.

"Are you ever planning on speaking again?" Stefan asked.

"Let's just get what we need and screw, all right? I got a bad feeling."

"Billy, for God's sake, it was just a bird. They fly into things sometimes."

"It's not just that. I don't like the looks of this place." He glanced around. "Notice anything strange about this town?"

"You mean besides the fact that Aunt Bea probably lives here?"

"Where the hell is everybody?"

Stefan scanned the area, taking it all in a moment. They were the only people on the street, and it was peculiarly quiet. "It is odd, but how many jobs could there be in a town this size? Most people probably work somewhere else, so in the middle of the day like this the place is basically empty."

"Yeah," Billy said reluctantly, "could be, I guess."

"Come on, let's have a look inside." Stefan motioned to the store. "If you're a good boy, I'll buy you an ice cream."

The gas station appeared as deserted as the rest of Boxer Hills. Not terribly well kept, the station's construction was most likely dated somewhere in the late 1940s or early 1950s. An old single pump sat out front in the dirt lot, and a wooden sign perched above the garage simply read: *Gas*. The main building was small but housed an office with an adjacent one-bay garage.

As Alex and Tory approached, they saw that the office door was open, but no one was inside. She poked her head in to be sure.

The office was cramped, cluttered and consisted of a desk covered in old, grease-stained paperwork, a counter area on which sat an antique cash register, an ancient telephone and a chipped coffee mug with spent cigarette butts floating in it, and a few folding chairs that constituted a waiting area of sorts. From the look of the place, no one had stepped foot within these walls in quite some time.

"They're obviously open," Alex said. "Somebody must be here."

They walked back outside and around to the garage bay. The door was raised, revealing a typical concrete floor and walls covered with an array of car parts, accessories and various tools and rags. But again, no sign of anyone.

"Maybe they're on break or something." Tory moved toward the rear of the building. "If there's a pooper, it's probably around back anyway."

They walked along the side of the garage until they reached a yard of overgrown weeds, assorted debris and trash, and a bevy of old, rusted-out automobile carcasses.

A filthy and battered door on the back wall of the garage

read: *Restroom*, the letters carved directly into the wood.

"Bogus!" Tory snorted.

Alex cringed, imagining what the inside of that bathroom looked like. "On second thought, maybe I can hold it a little while longer."

"Sorry, not me, I need to drain Monsignor Lizard-o immediately." Tory unzipped his fly, pulled himself free and shot an arc of urine into the air.

"Lovely. I'll meet you out front."

Alex turned and ran directly into a man in filthy overalls.

Startled, she jumped back. "Oh my God, I'm sorry," she said, laughing nervously. "You scared me, I didn't see you there."

The man's sleepy, bloodshot eyes shifted to Tory. "Just what in the *hell* you think you're doin'?"

In the sweetest voice she could muster, Alex answered for him. "We wanted to use your bathroom, but there wasn't anyone in the office."

Ignoring her, the man cocked his head. His mouth fell open to reveal a set of dark and rotting gums. "You pissin' on my station?"

Tory zipped up and moved to Alex's side. "Nah, it's not like that, bro, I didn't hit the building."

The man scratched his dirty neck with equally dirty fingers then ran a hand across his grimy, shaved dome of a head. Though it was difficult to gauge his age, he was most likely in his fifties. Tall and lean, he wore no shirt beneath the overalls, and his bronze skin had a leathery look often found in men who work outside for long periods in the sun. But in his present state it was difficult to tell where the filth ended and the tan began. "You read?"

"Huh?"

"*Read*," the man said. "Can you read?"

Tory grinned like an imbecile. "Sure."

He motioned to the bathroom door, lazily tossing his hand in its general direction. "Ain't you seen the restroom sign?"

"We're sorry," Alex said. "We didn't want to go in without permission so—"

"So, he figured he'd piss on my property like a dog?"

"I didn't mean any disrespect," Tory assured him. "Seriously, dude."

The man's eyes dropped the length of Tory's body, taking in the cutoff shorts, flip-flops, tie-dyed T-shirt, long blond hair and straw cowboy hat. "You with the carnival? What the hell kinda getup is that?" He gave Alex a sideways glance. Eye makeup, short black hair, loud sweatshirt. "And what're you 'posed to be, some sorta whore of Babylon?"

Alex blanched. "Excuse me?"

The man licked his chapped lips. "Why don't you pull them panties down and pee, too?"

"Hey, *bud*," Tory said, stepping forward, "be cool, *comprende*?"

In the time she'd known him, Alex had never before seen Tory exhibit anything close to anger, and though his attempt at chivalry was well-meaning, she also realized it could escalate things unless the situation was quickly defused. "Look, our friends are over at the general store," she told the man. "We'll go get them and come back and buy some gas from you, OK?"

The man casually pawed one of his large ears and appeared to consider what Alex had said longer than seemed warranted.

"We're really very sorry about this, sir," she added.

An unsettling smile slithered across his face. "We all outta gas."

"Bummer." Tory took Alex by the arm. "Let's vamoose."

A small bell jangled over the door as Stefan and Billy made their way into the general store. The ceiling was low and the floors consisted of an old wood plank design that looked as old as the building itself. Several rows of iron wire racks containing various items lined the main section of the store, and a counter sat near the bay window, an old cash register atop it and a man in his seventies standing behind it. He turned and looked at them as they entered but said nothing. In front of the counter stood another man about the same age who appeared to be visiting with the clerk. Both men clutched mugs of steaming coffee.

"Afternoon," Stefan said through a smile.

The men stared at them.

"Great," Billy muttered, approaching the counter. "Can I get a pack of Marlboro Box, please?"

"Ain't got that," the man said evenly.

Billy forced a smile. "Well, whatcha got, partner?"

"Luckies, Camel, Viceroy." The man pointed to a cardboard display ad at the end of the counter which showed the legendary Hollywood movie star Tyrone Power in an ascot and dinner jacket holding a cigarette. "And Chesterfield."

"I'll take the Luckies." Billy motioned to the counter ad. "That's pretty cool. Don't see that kind of thing much anymore."

The old man considered him a moment then slowly reached behind him to a low shelf, pulled free the cigarettes and tossed them on the counter.

Stefan headed down one of the aisles. He'd been hoping for a deli or something similar, but the store only carried the most basic groceries and a few items normally found in hardware stores. Odd thing was, everything looked wildly dated, and he'd never seen most of the brands. Those he had looked like vintage versions. He settled on an aisle with candy bars and decided to grab some to hold everyone over until they found a restaurant. But when he looked at them more closely, he realized they were all covered in a thin film of dust. He moved on, walking up and down each aisle. More of the same, everything was coated with dust.

At the counter, as Billy dug his wallet from his jeans, he noticed a magazine display a few feet away. It housed mostly hunting and fishing publications, as well as a detective magazine, a science fiction digest and a copy of *Life*. Each bore a publication date from 1947. Though they were coated with dust, they appeared to be in pristine condition. "Are these originals or reprints?"

"They just magazines is all." The old man remained expressionless. "You want anything 'sides the cigarettes?"

Billy looked back over his shoulder in time to find Stefan moving toward the counter with a confused expression. "You all set?"

"Completely."

"Just the butts then, chief," Billy said.

The man hit a key on the register. "Twenty cent."

Billy exchanged puzzled glances with Stefan then placed a quarter on the counter. "Keep the change. You gentlemen have a nice day now."

The man behind the counter nodded. His friend sipped his coffee with a loud slurp.

Once back outside on the front steps, Stefan grabbed Billy's arm. "Did you see how everything in there was covered in dust?"

"Yeah, what a dump. Scintillating counter help, too. Him and his buddy there, couple of charmers."

They moved down the steps together. "Billy, nothing in that store's been touched in God knows how long. It's like it's been closed for years and just reopened or something."

"You get a load of the magazine rack?" Billy tore open the pack of Lucky Strikes, pulled a cigarette free. "Everything in it's from 1947. I shit you not."

"That's thirty-six years ago. Why would they have magazines that old?"

"Why would he sell me a pack of butts for twenty cents and have an ad for Chesterfields with *Tyrone-fucking-Power* on his counter?" He lit the cigarette with his Zippo, took a hard drag and exhaled through his nose. "Let's just find the others and get back on the highway. This place gives me the creeps."

Alex and Tory appeared around the side of the gas station and moved quickly across the street. They all met at the Fairlane.

"You would *not* believe this guy we ran into over there," Alex said, checking over her shoulder to make certain they hadn't been followed.

"Wanna bet?" Billy took another pull on the cigarette, dropped it to the dirt and crushed it with the toe of his boot as Stefan and Alex exchanged stories. "I've heard enough. We're outta here."

As they opened the car doors, Stefan looked back at the general store. The bay window, segregated into small square panes, reflected the sunshine and made it impossible to see beyond the glass to the store inside. But something in one pane in particular caught his attention. An odd glare and then...

movement. He removed his sunglasses, rubbed his eyes and looked again. "What is that?"

The others followed his gaze to the window.

Inexplicably, the glass pane moved, rippling like water within its small frame before slightly bowing outward.

They watched it, dumbfounded, struck to silence and unable to fully comprehend what they were seeing. For several seconds, the glass undulated then settled and fell still, blending with the other panes and the rest of the window.

"That's not possible," Alex said dully.

"Let's get the hell out of here," Stefan said. "Come on, move!"

They frantically scrambled into the car.

Stefan turned the engine, dropped the shift into reverse and slammed the gas, spinning the tires in the dirt lot and kicking up a cloud of dust before rocketing back onto pavement. Rubber screeched, and the Fairlane shot down the main drag, back the way they'd come, hurtling in the direction of the highway at breakneck speed.

Trees flew past in a blur on either side of them as Stefan maneuvered the car along the winding road. "There must be an onramp somewhere in here."

"Look for that big town sign," Alex said. Relegated again to the back seat, she leaned forward. "It should be right along here, but slow down before you get us all killed, you'll—there—there it is!"

"What happened back there?" Tory asked, voice shaking. "How did the glass do that? How did it *move* like that?"

No one answered.

Instead, the Fairlane skidded to an abrupt halt next to the town sign.

To their right lay thick, nearly impenetrable forest.

The road they had taken off the highway, the one that had led them to Boxer Hills, was gone.

Chapter Four

"Where the hell's the road?" Billy pivoted in his seat. "It was right here."

"No *way*," Tory said, hands on his head.

Alex fidgeted about like a trapped animal. "How is this possible, we—"

"Everyone calm down," Stefan said in a controlled tone. "Let's all just take a deep breath. We're lost, that's all. We're not where we thought we were."

"The road was right across from that sign."

"Then this can't be the same sign."

"What about that shit with the window?" Tory asked.

"Sometimes the sun can hit glass and cause optical illusions due to the angle. It had to be a trick of the light."

"Cut the crap," Alex snapped, sitting forward. "We all know what we saw. You were as scared as the rest of us, Speed Racer."

"I'm just saying I think we overreacted."

"And I'm just saying I know what I saw, and what I saw wasn't..."

"Possible?"

"Well...yeah."

Stefan wiped perspiration from his brow with the back of his hand. "Look, we're tired, hungry and more than a little road weary. We let our imaginations get the better of us."

"Whatever, just keep driving," Billy said. "This road's got to come out somewhere, and sooner or later we're bound to run into signs for the highway."

Stefan drove on, this time at a slower and more reasonable speed. Though he continued to pretend he was relaxed and in control, he kept both hands on the wheel so no one would notice how badly they were shaking.

In relative silence, they followed the winding, heavily wooded road for several miles, passing occasional residences scattered throughout the forest. Most were literal shacks in various stages of disrepair, others more legitimate houses but still quite dated and modest.

Oddly, they saw no signs of life.

It was Tory who first noticed something else. Almost all the houses had small mirrors of some description either mounted or positioned in at least one window, facing outward, the reflective side aimed at the road.

"It's probably some peculiar local custom," Stefan said.

"Or you know what?" Alex jibed. "Maybe they're optical illusions!"

"Actually, there are lots of superstitions concerning mirrors." This from Billy, his eyes trained on the road before them.

"What is it with you and superstition all of a sudden?" Stefan said.

"My grandmother had tons of them. I grew up hearing the stories."

"Well, that nonsense is the last thing we need to worry about right now."

"Speak for yourself," Alex said. "What does it mean, Billy?"

"Putting a mirror in a window like that, facing out, has something to do with warding off evil spirits. I don't remember the exact specifics, but it's something along the lines of how a demon is so repulsive to the eye even its own reflection will repel it."

"Sounds about the right speed for the people we've run into so far." Stefan shook his head. "Welcome to Boxer Hills, gateway to the seventeenth century."

As they made their way around one particularly sharp bend in the road, they came upon a diner. A classic dining car design, the small building was wrapped in stainless steel and sported a neon sign on the roof that read: *Eats*. The parking lot was empty, and though the diner was far from pristine, it did appear to be open. "This place doesn't look *too* revolting." Stefan mustered a smile. "Want to give it a try?"

"Pull in," Alex said. "I have to pee so bad I can taste it."

Stefan slowed the car. They crept into the lot.

"I know nobody asked," Tory muttered restlessly, "but I say we get out of here and find us a tasty bit of choice highway instead."

"Relax, that town was hardly a sprawling metropolis," Stefan said. "We just covered a good ten miles. I seriously doubt we're even in Boxer Hills anymore."

"But you're not sure, are you?"

Stefan parked the Fairlane and killed the engine, the mirror image of the diner reflected in the dark lenses of his sunglasses. "No."

The smell of fried foods and freshly brewed coffee hung in the air. A row of stools and a counter area filled the back wall of the diner, a partially open kitchen behind them. A few booths lined the opposite wall, and the narrow passage between the two led to a payphone and restrooms at the rear of the eatery. Like much of what they'd seen before, the diner appeared to have been transported to 1983 from some earlier era. A middle-aged woman in a yellow waitress uniform and a white apron stood behind the counter, a pencil behind her ear. Behind her, a grizzled gray-haired man in whites moved about the kitchen. Three women on stools at the end of the counter, the only other customers in the place, looked up as they entered.

"Sit wherever you'd like," the waitress said, her voice raspy from too many cigarettes over too many years.

Stefan, Billy and Tory took up position on stools at the counter, and Alex hurried off to the bathroom. The waitress slid menus in front of them just as the cook hit a bell behind her. She turned, scooped up three plates of food and brought them to the women at the end of the counter.

Alex returned from the restroom a moment later and joined the others at the counter. While she, Stefan and Tory scanned their menus, Billy studied the women. He guessed it was a mother and two daughters, though the mother looked relatively young. Early forties, he thought, and the daughters late teens. All three were attractive but heavily made-up, their hairdos out of date and frozen in place with copious amounts of hairspray. Even their clothes were bizarre, dresses and shoes he'd only seen people wear in old movies. The women noticed him looking their way and smiled in turn.

Billy pretended to read the menu.

"Can you believe how cheap these prices are?" Alex said softly.

Stefan nodded. "Just like the general store."

"Ma'am, what town is this?" Tory asked the waitress as she moved past.

"Boxer Hills."

"We're just passing through," Stefan said, ignoring Tory's laser stare, "on our way to Bar Harbor."

"Glad you found us," she said with a wry smile, her teeth stained brown from years of black coffee, cigarettes and neglect.

"So what's good today?"

"Best burgers and iced tea in the state of Maine," she said flatly.

"Then that's what I'll have."

Billy was still watching the women. "The same," he said absently.

"Yeah," Tory mumbled, "me too."

The waitress removed a pad from her apron, jotted down their orders then eyed Alex. "And you?"

"The same but with an ice water, please."

As the waitress moved away, Stefan leaned closer to Tory, who was spinning back and forth on his stool like a child trying to effectively watch every corner of the diner at once. "Will you knock it off?"

"We're still in—"

"Everything's fine. Let's just eat and we'll go. Relax."

Billy lit a cigarette and again glanced at the women. The youngest, a brunette with expressive blue eyes, her lips painted with bright lipstick, smiled coyly and batted her eyelashes. This time he smiled back.

"Um, ew," Alex said under her breath. "Try to keep it in

your pants for once, would you, sport?"

Stefan gave a comical grimace. "Nobody told me The Andrew Sisters were going to be here."

But for Tory, who had no idea who The Andrew Sisters were, they all laughed and began to feel more at ease with their surroundings.

As they waited for the food, for the first time since the freak rainstorm they began to enjoy themselves, engaging in small talk and banter. In time it seemed Stefan had been right after all. Maybe they had let their imaginations run wild. Maybe Boxer Hills was just an odd little town in the middle of nowhere that was a throwback to an earlier era, a village that had hung on to the past and become set in its ways. Maybe it was that simple.

The waitress eventually delivered their lunches. As she moved away, Billy again made eye contact with the women. The youngest ran her tongue across her lips suggestively.

"Well, this looks good," Stefan said with his best attempt at cheeriness. He held the burger in both hands and took a generous bite.

Thick splotches of bright red blood exploded from it, spraying the counter area and his plate. Stefan dropped the sandwich and staggered back off his stool, hands furiously wiping the crimson from his mouth. "What the hell is this," he gasped, shaking dollops of blood from his hands, "what—what did you give me?"

The meat bounced off the counter and fell to the floor with a nauseating splat, more blood and viscera flying from it. The gray, loosely formed meat was drenched in blood, and what Stefan had previously thought chopped onions, were in fact slowly writhing maggots.

"Jesus!" Alex screamed and jumped to her feet.

Billy had seen what happened, but still mesmerized by the women, did not move. Their smiles slowly faded, their faces turned serious and cold, and previously enticing stares became masks of intensity. Though it disturbed him on a level primal in its depth, the shift in the women was so sudden and extreme he could not take his eyes from them. He'd never seen anything quite like it.

Stefan gagged then began to cough.

By the time Alex had gone to him with a napkin and wiped the remnants of blood from his face, the cough had escalated to violent choking. He stumbled back a few feet, hands to his throat.

"Gnarly, dude," Tory said, moving toward him, "you all right?"

"Stef?" Alex put her hand on his back. "He's choking—he's—he's choking! What the hell did you give him?"

Billy, still entranced with the women, watched as they continued to glare.

Stefan's choking became worse.

"He can't breathe!" Alex cried.

Her shriek snapped Billy free of his trance, and he quickly went to Stefan's side as well. He pounded on his back but it did no good. He asked him what he was choking on, but when Stefan attempted an answer, a thick drool of spittle uncoiled from his mouth and dangled in a long string nearly to the floor. As his upper body bucked, he vomited. Hands pawing at his throat, Stefan's face grew blood red.

"Call an ambulance!" Billy said, turning to the waitress. She stared at him. "Now, goddamn it! Do it now!"

The cook came out from the kitchen, a cleaver in hand, and watched as well, his face expressionless. Neither made a move to help.

Billy turned to the women. They were smiling again, pleased. "What the hell is wrong with you people?"

Stefan's legs buckled, but Alex and Tory were there to catch him. Still unable to draw air, he began to convulse and writhe about, his eyes bulging grotesquely.

"He's choking to death!" Alex grabbed hold of him and tried desperately to see into his throat, but nothing seemed to be blocking his airway. "Call a fucking ambulance!"

Billy spun and slammed a fist into the center of Stefan's chest.

He gagged, vomited a second time then dropped to his knees and drew a sudden intake of air so violent it manifested as an audible screech.

Alex knelt next to him and gently rubbed his back. "It's OK, just breathe. Nice deep breaths, that's it."

With a crazed expression, the cook suddenly swung the cleaver and buried it in the counter with a loud thud.

They all jumped, startled and confused.

The women at the counter began to laugh, but there was no humor in it, no joy. It was laughter so scornful and vicious it froze Billy's blood in his veins.

"Get him up and outside," Billy said, hands at his side but clenched into fists.

As Alex and Tory helped Stefan to the door, Billy grabbed the car keys from the counter and followed them, moving backward so he could keep the townspeople in his line of sight.

"Go ahead, run." The waitress smiled, flashing her brown teeth. "You're not *going* anywhere."

Chapter Five

"**G**et him in the car," Billy said. "I'll drive."

Still holding Stefan steady, Alex and Tory hurriedly maneuvered him into the back seat. Tory slid in next to him and Alex took shotgun. "What did that mean?" she asked as Billy climbed behind the wheel. "What did she mean, *we're not going anywhere?*"

"These people, they—they're just fucking with us."

"Why?"

"I don't know, but we're not hanging around to find out."

"What the hell was that?" Tory said hysterically. "What did that bitch serve us, they—the blood, the—it looked like human blood, and the shit falling off it—"

"It doesn't make any sense," Alex interrupted. "We haven't done anything to them, why would they do this?"

Rather than engage in further conversation, Billy sped from the lot and continued in the same direction they'd been heading when they came upon the diner. Nervously checking the rearview every few seconds, he was certain if they put enough distance between themselves and Boxer Hills proper, they'd eventually cross the town line or again gain access to the state highway.

But the farther they drove the more remote the area became.

Before, where they had seen an occasional house or street sign, they now saw only trees and increasingly aged, decayed pavement, the forest on either side of them thicker, deeper, darker.

"How you holding up back there?" Billy asked.

"I'm totally not into this," Tory said.

"I meant Stefan, moron."

"My throat's sore, but I'm OK," he said, voice raspy.

"The road's gone to shit." Billy slowed the car. The condition of the road was suddenly so bad it had become dangerous to proceed at anything beyond a crawl. "Christ, we're in the middle of nowhere."

He made a three-point turn and headed back in the opposite direction. They soon passed the diner, but again, saw no roads for the highway, and eventually found themselves back in downtown Boxer Hills.

"Sonofabitch," Billy muttered as the car rolled to a stop. "You gotta be kidding me."

Alex pointed to another side road off Main Street. "There, try that one."

Billy did, following yet another country road along a winding path that went on for several minutes only to empty out right back where they'd started, at the beginning of Main Street.

"Every goddamn road dumps us right back here."

"We just went in a completely different direction," Alex said wearily. "How could we end up in the exact same spot?"

Stefan massaged his temples. "What the hell's happening?"

"All these roads look the same." Billy sighed. "We've got to be missing something, there has to be a way out of here."

"It'd be tubular if you could find it." Tory pushed his cowboy hat down tighter on his head. "Because sincerely, I'm having a cow, I'm totally giving birth."

Billy watched the main drag awhile.

No people. No cars. No animals.

Madness.

Once again, he headed for the road that had brought them here.

Nearly half an hour later, after driving in every direction and taking every road they could find, they continued to wind up in exactly the same place. All roads led to this single destination, as if the town of Boxer Hills had somehow been cordoned off from the rest of the planet the moment they crossed into it. And impossible as it seemed—impossible as it had to be—after exhaustive attempts and numerous arguments, they finally had no choice but to accept that there truly was no way out.

The waitress's words had proven prophetic after all.

You're not going anywhere.

Billy parked on the side of the road at the mouth of Main Street. "I don't...I don't understand."

"Now what?" Alex asked, emotion straining her voice.

Billy took her hand and gave it a reassuring squeeze. For weeks he'd watched her act terrified, playing at horror onstage. It had been a terribly draining process, and often after their performances he'd spent an hour or two decompressing and clearing his mind of the hideous images of fear his character had inflicted upon her. Assuming the role of a heartless psychopath night after night was emotionally exhausting enough, but when it was aimed at someone he truly cared for, psychologically, it was downright excruciating. And this new look of terror on her face was even worse because there was no premeditated method behind it. This was no hoax made to appear real, an illusion they both knew and understood the inner workings of. These emotions were genuine, deadly, and all Billy could see was a young woman he knew and loved and respected, a woman who had once been a lover but who would always be a friend, there for him even when he stumbled, even when he fell, someone who championed him though he rarely deserved to be. In his brief twenty-one years he'd already garnered a reputation as someone unreliable and sure to disappoint more often than not. He'd spent what little life he'd had letting people down and falling short. This time it would be different. "Everything's gonna be fine," he told her. "Trust me. I'll get us out of here."

She nodded rapidly, as if fervor alone might make it so. "OK."

"None of this makes any sense," Stefan said quietly, and then, as if it had only just occurred to him, "I could've choked to death back there, I could've died. I thought I *was* dying. It felt so strange, like someone was strangling me."

"Those women acted like they were making it happen," Billy said, "like they were controlling it."

"That's ridiculous."

"So is trying to feed us whatever the fuck that was they gave us. So is every road in this town leading us right back here. So is the road that brought us here in the first place vanishing into thin air."

"Let's not lose our minds," Stefan said. "We need to stay clearheaded."

"Nothing's been right since that storm. Nothing's been normal since."

"Do you honestly think I'm unaware of that?" Stefan dropped his head. "I just…I don't know what to make of any of this."

Billy watched the trees lining Main Street, so perfect and uniform, so falsely beautiful. What was this place, what was it really, truly, behind the façade? "For some reason, this town won't let us leave," he said, angrily pushing open the car door. "Let's go find out why."

With Billy in the lead, the quartet left the car on the outskirts of Main Street and walked toward the center of town. The park and gazebo on the first block were empty. The post office that followed was closed, and the police station next door sat vacant. As they ventured farther, marching right up the middle of the street, they saw that the general store had also been shut down. Everything was abandoned. What few townspeople had been there previously had seemingly locked up and walked away.

"When's the last time you saw a police station close?" Billy asked. The heels of his scuffed boots clacked pavement, and as he keyed on the cadence, something else occurred to him. He came to a stop. The others did the same. "Listen. There aren't even any birds singing. None in the sky, either."

"I haven't seen an animal since we got here," Alex said. "Not even a bug."

"Are you guys sure getting out of the car is a good idea?" Tory asked. "That dude with the cleaver wasn't joking."

"We don't have much choice at this point." Billy looked back in the direction they'd come. The Fairlane and the false sense of safety it represented sat undisturbed, the street behind them empty. The others awaited his next move. Stefan massaged his throat, looking more drained and overwhelmed than Billy had ever seen him. In his IZOD shirt, shorts and penny loafers, he looked like some displaced catalogue model. Tory shuffled about uneasily, that silly hat in place and a joint he still hadn't smoked cradled behind his ear. Closest to Billy stood Alex, the fiery determination in her big brown eyes not quite capable of concealing her fear, her sweatshirt hanging loosely to reveal a small, smooth shoulder, the delicate skin there flaked from recent sunburn.

Billy could only wonder what they saw when they looked at him.

A gentle but warm breeze kicked up and blew across the road, rustling the trees lining either side of it before continuing on to the forest. The sun had become partially obscured by a bank of gray clouds rolling ominously across the horizon, and humidity was on the rise, converting the previously dry and comfortable heat into one far more oppressive and sticky.

"It's gonna rain again," Tory said listlessly. "What's with this weather?"

Billy walked on. The others followed.

They moved past the general store to the street beyond. The firehouse was unattended, and there was no sign of the man in overalls or anyone else at the gas station. The windowless stone structure at the end of the street—a building they had assumed was a church—was quiet. That left only the library. Though there were no signs of life coming from it either, the front doors were open. A plaque which read *Alton Boxer Public Library* hung over the front entrance. Billy hesitated just shy of the quaint gravel path leading to the front doors. Despite its small size, the multi-peaked roof and formal front porch gave the building a decidedly colonial flavor. Painted bright white and beautifully landscaped, it was, rather ironically, the best-kept and most attractive piece of property in town.

Thunder rumbled in the distance, piercing the silence.

"There's a lot of useful information in a library," Alex said, her voice echoing along the lonely street. "You know, town history, general info, that sort of thing? And there are usually maps."

The library stood before them, offering nothing, its open doors an invitation or a trap, a portal to understanding or a predator poised to devour them.

"Except for this place everything in town's shut down tight," Billy said. "That's no accident. There's something in here they want us to see."

They stepped into a wide foyer. A winding staircase to their right led to a second floor, a no admittance sign on a small chain strung across it signaling everything other than the main floor was off limits to the public. Several portraits of stern-faced men and dour women in colonial garb—evidently prominent people in the town's history—haunted the walls of the foyer, hanging in matching antique frames and glowering at Billy and the others from their distant pasts like the intruders they were. Numerous book displays, mostly dog-eared paperbacks and magazines on free-standing racks, led to another open doorway and the main library area, which was small and somewhat cramped.

Tall bookcases packed to capacity lined the walls, and a basic wooden table and chairs occupied the center of the room. A set of lofty windows along the back wall revealed a view of a pleasantly landscaped yard area and an expanse of forest beyond. Beneath one window sat a glass case containing what appeared to be older, perhaps more valuable books, and an unexceptional assortment of town artifacts. The librarian's desk was unoccupied, but amidst a small stack of paperwork, a few books and an outmoded telephone, a cup of coffee sat at its front right corner, still steaming.

"Whoa," Tory said. "Look at that dude."

On an interior wall behind them hung another portrait, this one larger than the others and housed in a gold-leaf frame. It bore the steely likeness of a gaunt man in later middle age. Dressed in a dark robe, his arms held out to his sides, palms up, he stared down at them with furious condemnation. His fiery eyes, receding shock of black hair and bony face made for a presence equal parts mesmerizing and deeply unsettling. On a small gold plate mounted beneath the portrait *The Reverend Alton Boxer, 1699* had been inscribed.

"Must be the town's founder," Billy said.

"Charming," Stefan said.

Billy watched the eyes in the portrait. There was a sickness to them, something dark and depraved. A chill licked his spine, slowly inching up toward the back of his neck. He forced himself away, deeper into the room.

As the others separated, taking in various areas of the library, Billy moved to one wall of bookcases. As he scanned the titles, the scope of the section began to take shape. The entire side wall of the library was dedicated to the occult. "Guys, you better take a look at this."

Stefan, once aware of what he was seeing, gave a resigned sigh. "Great."

"Why would a town this small have such a huge number of books on occultism?" Alex asked. "Half the library's nothing but."

"Look at some of the titles," Billy said, reading the spines. "There are lots of books about town history in this section too, so I think it's safe to assume the people here are tied to this sort of thing."

"And always have been," Alex added.

"Maybe it's a religious thing," Stefan said, "a sect or something."

"Not all occult stuff's bad." Tory leaned against the corner of the table. "It covers a lot of area, actually. I dated this one really cool Wiccan chick from Frisco and she was—"

"Yeah, fascinating, but that's not what this is." Billy selected a few titles then brought them to the table. "Let's see what these have to say."

The first book, published in the early 1940s, had been written by a local schoolteacher and centered mostly on town history. Flipping through the pages, Billy came upon a chapter dedicated to town founder Alton Boxer. The first page showed a drawing of him standing at the mouth of a large field, his black robes flowing in the wind, one hand pointing toward distant hills and the other clutching a bible of some kind. Behind him, a group of stone-faced settlers gazed at the horizon. "This Boxer cat was a minister from Massachusetts," Billy said, reading the page of text opposite. "In 1691 he and his followers were charged with heresy, witchcraft and consorting with the Devil. They were thrown out of the church, but Boxer and his flock took off before they could be tried. This is where they ended up."

"Sixteen ninety-one," Alex echoed. "A year later all hell broke out in Massachusetts. Miller's *The Crucible* anyone?"

"But the Salem Witch Trials were nothing more than mass hysteria," Stefan reminded them. "It wasn't real."

"Doesn't mean this guy wasn't," Billy said, scanning the next page. "Ten years before the trials in Salem, New Castle Island in New Hampshire was plagued by mysterious demonic events, including hundreds of stones that fell from the heavens. The culprit was Lithobolia, the stone-throwing devil. Many believed this is where it all began, and that these events are what led to the strange happenings in Massachusetts. The Devil was on the loose, roaming from place to place. Alton Boxer visited New Castle while those events were happening. He had gone there as a man of God to investigate the alleged satanic forces at play himself, but soon returned to Massachusetts to tend to his church. For several years afterward, Boxer struggled with his faith and began to secretly investigate and study the occult. During this period, his teachings slowly began to change and embrace a different philosophy. According to this, through his studies of the occult he came to understand 'the truth'. He'd seen it, this says. Boxer saw evil incarnate, its existence to him no longer a matter of faith but proven reality. He and his followers came to believe that purity could only truly be gained through total and absolute submission to sin."

"Pure evil," Stefan said.

"He taught that physical immortality for human beings was possible, but that it could not be gained through service to God. It could only be obtained by submitting to Man's greatest adversary." Billy looked up from the book, face pale. "Lucifer."

"Fuuuuck," Tory said, "they're a bunch of Devil freaks, dude."

"At least their founders were." Alex leaned forward, both hands on the table. "What happened to this Boxer character?"

"Doesn't say." Billy flipped through the book. "He founded

the town in 1692, but I don't see anything in here about Boxer's death." He closed the book, put it aside and moved to the next, an autobiography on an Italian man named Dante Salerno, an evidently well-known spiritualist and practitioner of the black arts who had apparently visited Boxer Hills in the 1940s. On the title page, Salerno had autographed the book and written the following inscription: *To the people of Boxer Hills. Thank you for your warm welcome and hospitality. I dedicate this book to you, and all followers of the truth.—Eternally, Dante Salerno, August 1946.* Billy relayed it then read from the biography. "Apparently this guy was a celebrity of sorts in occult circles. Sounds like an Aleister Crowley type. Seems odd that this guy would come to a town as small and remote as Boxer Hills, but this place obviously held significance for him." He rifled through the third book he'd chosen, a book on séances, and then the forth, a history of angels, including the fallen, but didn't find anything relevant. "What's really weird is that all these books were published before 1947, so they don't mention anything beyond that year. That in itself isn't strange, but if you think about it, from the moment we got here we haven't come across a single thing outside that timeframe. It's like time's stopped in this town."

"But why 1947?" Alex asked. "Why that year specifically?"

Billy pushed the stack of books away, sliding them to the far edge of the table. "I don't know."

"OK, well obviously time standing still isn't possible, so it has to be something simpler than that." Stefan began to pace on the opposite side of the table. "Maybe, like I said before, this is some sort of cult town, a religious sect into some far out dogma who for some reason feel the need to keep Boxer Hills tied to its past, to keep it frozen in 1947 rather than allowing it to move forward into the present."

"This isn't about possible or impossible anymore." Billy rose from his chair at the table. "What's it gonna take to get that through your head?"

"Some things have happened, but we can't—"

"For Christ's sake, the people at that diner tried to serve us what very well may have been part of a human being!"

"We don't know that, it could've been—"

"You almost choked to death! You almost died!"

"Thanks so much for letting me know. I had no idea when I was vomiting and couldn't breathe that I was in any danger whatsoever."

"Both of you be quiet," Alex said suddenly, holding her hand up. "Listen."

Through the open library doors came a soft and distant sound. Though the specific words were garbled, the delivery was consistent and repetitive, like chanting. Slowly, it grew louder then louder still.

Somewhere nearby, a large group of people had begun to pray.

Chapter Six

They emerged from the library, followed the gravel path out to the road then moved toward the stone building at the end of the street. The gray sky had turned darker, littered with enormous black storm clouds that churned slowly beyond the tops of the trees and blotted out any memory of sunshine. The humidity remained. The praying, a deep and eerie monotone, grew louder the closer they got to it, and like sailors mesmerized by a siren's song, Billy led the others across the property. The sound reminded him of a radio program his grandmother listened to when he was a child. Early in the morning the station had broadcast monks reciting the rosary. His grandmother would sit in her favorite chair and say her rosary with them, and Billy was always drawn to the droning, emotionless voices. As they echoed through the ancient cathedral, Billy often attempted to visualize these men in his mind, conjuring shadowy figures in brown robes, hoods concealing their faces as candlelight flickered against the dark and dreary stone walls of their monastery. Sometimes he even sat on the floor near his grandmother's chair and whispered along.

These prayers, however, were unlike any Billy had ever heard.

A dirt path cut through the square of grass yard in front of the church. There were no markings of any kind on the building. The structure itself looked quite old but sturdy, constructed of dark stone to form something similar in appearance to a chapel. Atop the roof, where a cross or some other religious signature normally would have stood, lay only a small steeple of rock.

The front door, a slab of thick wood with a black iron ring in place of a knob, bore no clues as to the building's identity either, but it was streaked with a thin bloody stain that ran from its center to the bottom of the doorway.

"Are you sure this is a church?" Alex asked.

"Whatever, I'm not going in there." Tory, who had stayed at the rear of the group, took a step back out toward the road. "You saw what those books said. They're probably sacrificing babies and shit."

Stefan stuffed his hands in his pockets. "Maybe we should just leave, get back on the road and—"

"Drive around in circles?" Billy shook his head. "There's a storm bearing down on us and it'll be night soon. I don't want to be here after dark."

Tory paced about anxiously. "What the hell language are they speaking?"

"Latin," Alex said.

"Well, obviously," Stefan cracked. "But do you know what they're saying?"

"Sorry, only took one semester of it in high school."

"Fuck this shit." Billy grabbed hold of the black iron ring and pulled. The heavy door opened with a scraping sound, its bottom edge grazing the stone base of the doorway as he flung it back and stepped over the threshold.

The prayers ceased, and but for a murmur of outlying thunder, the town of Boxer Hills had again fallen silent.

A musty smell wafted from inside the church, billowing out through the doorway. The interior was dusty, unkempt, and consisted of several wooden pews positioned along the stone floor and an altar at the rear of the building that appeared quite old and bore no religious markings. It was all quite sparse, dark and unremarkable.

The church was also completely empty.

"Where are the people?" It was the third time Tory had asked the question since Billy opened the door.

Finally, Stefan attempted an answer. "Could it have been a tape or—"

"Stefan, enough, OK?" Alex ran her hands through her hair. "Enough."

"But there has to be a reasonable explanation."

Billy moved deeper inside the church. It looked as if it had been empty for years. He walked toward the altar. A rock about the size of a grapefruit sat at its center, a withered and dried out piece of parchment pinned beneath it. He pushed the rock aside and pulled free the parchment. The upper right edge crumbled in his hands, falling away in dusty pieces to the floor. The remainder was an artist's rendition of what appeared to be a demonic court jester, half human, half devil, with a hideous grin that revealed razor-like teeth, one hand clutching its long, winding, reptilian-like tail, the other holding a stone. Behind it, two jagged leathery wings extended up like giant claws. "What's the demon that book talked about?" Billy asked. "The one Boxer went to investigate."

"Lithobolia," Alex said, "the stone-throwing devil."

Billy searched the thing's eyes. It appeared to be laughing at him. "I think that's what these people worship," he said, turning the aged paper so the others could see. "I think that's what this is."

"Whatever Boxer found in that New Hampshire town in 1692, it changed him," Alex said. "And he brought it back with him to Massachusetts. That's why he and his followers fled and came here, where it was secluded and private, where they could worship their god, a god of evil who promised immortality through dedication and submission to sin. The people in this town have probably worshipped Lithobolia for generations."

Tory poked his head through the doorway but refused to enter the church. "Are you guys insane? *Where* are the *people*?"

"Look around." Billy tossed the parchment back onto the altar as if it were riddled with disease. "There hasn't been anybody in this church in years."

"That can't be," Stefan mumbled. "We heard them praying, we heard them, it was no mistake, we—there *has* to be a reasonable explanation."

Billy left the altar and headed for the door, stopping next to Stefan. "You're like a brother to me, man, and I love you. But I swear to God, if you say that one more time, I'm gonna knock you the fuck out."

Nodding helplessly, Stefan wandered back outside.

Once he'd gone, Alex gave Billy's arm a gentle squeeze. "You know how Stef is. In his mind there's an answer for everything. As much of an artist as he is, he also believes deeply in science, reason and logic."

"And we don't?"

"Yes, we do, but we also believe in God, Billy, in an afterlife, the spiritual side of things. He doesn't. This shatters everything he thought he knew."

"It shatters everything we *all* thought we knew." Billy took a final look around the church. "Whatever's going on here is—"

"Hey, there's somebody coming!" Tory stumbled through the doorway, tripping his way into the church. "A tow truck's bringing a car to the gas station. That redneck dude in the overalls is driving, Alex."

"Tory," Billy said, looking past him, "where's Stefan?"

"He went to go talk to him."

Billy ran for the door.

A dilapidated tow truck was parked along the side of the gas station, a wood panel station wagon attached to its towing mechanism. The towed car only looked a few years old and was the first relatively modern thing they'd seen since entering Boxer Hills. The owners, however, were nowhere in sight.

As Billy and the others ran up the street toward the gas station, they saw that Stefan was already within a few feet of the truck. The man in overalls climbed down from the cab, his work boots kicking up a cloud of dust as they made contact with the dirt lot. Upon seeing Stefan, he stiffened, but when he noticed the others coming, he casually leaned against the tow truck door and wiped perspiration from his neck with a grimy handkerchief.

The sky had turned darker.

"—and we thought maybe you could help us," Stefan was saying as the others scrambled into the lot.

The man gave a contemptuous snort, his bloodshot eyes

narrowing when he saw Alex and Tory. "Carnival's back in town," he said, shifting his gaze to Stefan and Billy. "And this time they brung a city queer and a little punk with 'em."

"Mister, we don't want any trouble," Stefan said, "we just—"

"Fuck that." Billy pushed past him, stood directly in front of the man and stabbed a finger at him threateningly. "Listen up, *Dad*, you either tell me what the hell's going on right now or there's gonna be one less backwoods country fuck in this town, you got it?"

If the man was intimidated, he gave no indication. Slowly, he wiped the sweat from his neck as a toothless grin spread across his craggy face.

Stefan stepped between them. "There were people praying but the church was empty. Where did they go? The people, they—we *heard* them—what were they doing?"

"Preparin'," the man answered. "We all preparin'."

"Preparing?"

"For the gatherin'."

As the others exchanged uneasy glances, Tory drifted toward the station wagon for a closer look. Looking back, he noticed two men standing across the street in front of the general store. One held a pitchfork, the other a crowbar. Both were watching them.

"The gathering of what?"

Tory inched closer to the station wagon, stealing a glance farther up the road. Four more townspeople, three men and a woman, had taken up position at the end of Main Street. They stood watching with blank, emotionless faces.

The man stuffed the rag into his overalls. "Souls."

Rain began to fall, landing in big fat drops all around them, clanging against the gas pump, thudding in the dirt, drumming the roofs of the vehicles and blurring the windows in the buildings. Windows now filled with distorted faces. Men...women...children...

Tory looked over his shoulder. Another group of townspeople had appeared. Standing around the Fairlane, they, like the others, made no move toward them, preferring instead to stare like lifeless mannequins. He counted a total of twelve people on the street, but each time he looked in a different direction more appeared, emerging slowly from the buildings or walking out of the forest. He craned his neck, saw that another large group had collected in the park on the next block, and more still had filled the gazebo.

"Gathering souls?" Stefan asked frantically. "What does that mean?"

The man's smile receded. "Means you're all *fucked*."

"Look," Tory said in an unusually forceful tone.

The others turned to him, and in doing so, saw the townspeople.

"My God," Alex whispered.

The man began to laugh. "Your God's not here, bitch."

Billy grabbed him by the front of his overalls and slammed him into the truck, pinning him there. "Who are you people?"

Thunder exploded overhead, and the downpour intensified.

The station wagon now within reach, Tory placed a hand against the side panel and peered through the open windows.

"What do they want?" Like a zoo animal walking its cage, Stefan strode back and forth in a short space. "What do they want?"

Tory backed away from the car, the color drained from his face. "Run."

Alex traced his stare to the station wagon. She began to scream.

And then Billy and Stefan saw it too.

The interior of the car was smeared and spattered with blood.

Chapter Seven

By the time Billy realized the man in overalls had reached behind him and grabbed hold of something on the seat of the tow truck, it was too late. The man's hand was already swinging, coming down across the top of Billy's forearm in an arcing motion, and though he'd seen it clearly, it took a few seconds to register that the object in the man's hand was a rusty hunting knife. He felt no pain, only pressure followed by a burning sensation as he threw an elbow into the man's face. There was a sickening cracking sound, like the snap of a dried twig, and the man cried out, hands clutching his shattered nose. Not far behind him, Billy heard Alex scream, and other voices laced with urgency. He grabbed the back of the man's head with both hands, yanked it down so he was doubled-over, and thrust a knee up into his face. With a grunt, the man collapsed at Billy's feet, the knife falling from his grasp and bouncing away.

A fast-growing pool of blood leaked from beneath the man, seeping into and mixing with the dirt and rain to form a horrible maroon sludge.

"Jesus Christ!" Stefan, still unsure of what to do, jerked his head back and forth between Billy and the townspeople. "Did you kill him?"

Adrenaline pumping, Billy crouched down and grabbed the weapon, noticing that the wound on his forearm, a thin gash halfway up his arm, had just then begun to bleed. "Motherfucker cut me."

Alex moved toward him then seemed to change her mind and turned back, addressing the townspeople. "What the hell is wrong with you? Why are you doing this? What did we do to you? What do you want?"

Silent and motionless, the townspeople watched them.

"Answer me! What do you want? What the *fuck* do you want?"

Billy caught Stefan's eyes and cocked his head toward Alex, signaling him to go to her. He did, putting his arms around her, and though she struggled at first, she eventually calmed enough to understand he was trying to help her.

"Why won't they answer me?" she asked, spitting the words. "Why won't they answer me?"

"We gotta run for it." Tory straightened his cowboy hat and kicked off his flip-flops. "We gotta get to the car."

"There's too many of them." Billy motioned toward the Fairlane. A group of people now surrounded it. "But this truck runs."

Straddling the man in the dirt, Tory checked the ignition. "No keys."

"Shit." Billy knelt down. "Help me check his pockets."

Another thunderclap sounded, letting loose an even harder rain.

"Billy." With an arm still wrapped around Alex's shoulder, Stefan stepped back, pulling her with him and nearly tripping in the process. "Billy, they're coming."

Even before he looked up and saw the townspeople advancing through the rain, slowly at first and then faster, wave after wave surging toward them, many of them armed with various weapons, Billy knew there wouldn't be enough time to do anything but run. It was their only chance. He looked to the trees beyond the church. "There's an opening," he said. "There. Stay together and don't stop for anything. *Anything*, you hear me?" He rose to his feet, tucked the knife in his belt and drew a deep breath. "Go!"

They broke away from the truck, darted across the street and sprinted for the church, Billy in the lead, Tory close behind and Stefan and Alex at the rear but running hard.

The townspeople followed.

Blinking away rain, Billy's boots splashed puddles as he

crossed onto the church property and ran for the tree line. "Make it!" he called to the others, glancing behind him to make sure they were all still with him. "Make it!"

But in the split-second his head was turned, he didn't see the group of townspeople emerge from behind the church and run into their path, effectively blocking their escape through the forest.

"Bro, in front of you!" Tory called.

Led by a man carrying a hand scythe, it's curved blade raised high, six men, two women and a boy no more than eight or nine closed in on them.

Without slowing his stride, Billy pulled the knife from his belt and screamed, "Run right through them!"

With a scream somewhere between battle cry and terror, Tory leapt forward into the air, his bare foot colliding with the middle of one man's chest with such force it sent him hurdling backward to the ground. As Tory landed, two other men converged on him. Something grabbed his arm, yanked it violently as unseen fingers gripped his throat, scratched his face and tugged at his body. Arms flailing, he felt his fist connect with something solid and then he was free and running again. "Go!" he called to Stefan and Alex, who had already moved past the attackers and were nearly to the forest. "Go!"

Someone grabbed him from behind. Tory turned and awkwardly threw a punch, but now others had joined the fray and were converging on him at once, their hands clamping onto him from every angle, clawing and pulling him in various directions. Absorbed into their mass, he fell with a shriek of terror and agony, his final words pleas for mercy as he vanished in a sea of thrashing arms, stomping legs, swinging weapons and a spray of blood.

Billy ran directly for the man with the hand scythe. With a fierce slashing motion, he swung the blade between them, catching the man's face. The man fell to his knees in shock, dropped the scythe and fumbled at the gaping wound.

Before Billy could think about what he'd done, a second man came from behind him. He shifted his weight to his front foot and launched the other into the midsection of the man, sending him vaulting back just as a woman appeared, lunging at him and scratching at his eyes with a maniacal screech.

With a downward stroke, Billy buried the knife in her forehead. The blade connected with skull and snapped, breaking off near the handle, as the woman fell away in a mist of rain and crimson.

Just before he darted into the woods, Billy saw the other townspeople gathered around what remained of Tory. They continued to attack him with frenzied glee as more of their brethren ran through the streets and converged on the bloody scene.

Billy sprinted for the woods. Trying his best to avoid smashing headlong into the trees, behind him he could still hear the savage cries of the townspeople and the gut-wrenching sound of Tory being ripped limb from limb, his cracking bones and splitting flesh coupled with nearly orgasmic moans reverberating through the forest.

He couldn't be certain how far he'd run, but Billy continued on through the forest until his legs gave way and he tumbled down a slope to the base of a small stream. Bouncing along the rugged and uneven terrain, he rolled through the fall and came up on all fours, rainwater and remnants of blood bathing his face.

He looked behind him, listened.

Silence.

Something moved past the edge of his peripheral vision.

Stefan stumbled toward him from the other side of the stream. His pale face shown through the rain as he splashed across the shallow water then collapsed next to him. Behind him Alex materialized, chest heaving. Soaked, exhausted and in shock, the trio sat quietly in the forest, rain cutting through the trees all around them.

"They got Tory," Billy said. "He's dead."

"I don't believe this," Alex said, sobbing. "Why is this happening? *How* can this be happening?"

Billy headed to the stream, fell to his knees and splashed water on the cut along his forearm, doing his best to cleanse it.

Though the wound was long but not terribly deep, it continued to seep blood. Flashes of their pursuers attacking with hatchets, baseball bats, pitchforks, crowbars and anything else they'd managed to arm themselves with blinked across his mind's eye. "I killed one of them," he mumbled. "A woman, I...I was looking right in her eyes."

The knife blade clanging against skull echoed in memory.

"Tory's dead?" Stefan shook his head in disbelief. "He's really dead, you're sure?"

"I saw him go down. They killed him, they..."

"Why would they do this?"

"He saved my ass back there. If he hadn't called out and warned me, the ones who came at us from behind the church would've gotten me."

"You *killed* someone?" Stefan asked, as if it had only then registered.

Alex's sobbing turned suddenly to anger. "Why would they attack us like that? Why are they doing this? Why!"

"Keep your voice down, they're probably still on our asses." Billy struggled to his feet and did his best to force the emotion and fear away. "Let's go, get up. We've got to keep moving."

They followed the stream awhile, running when they had the wind and walking when they grew too tired. Although they neither saw nor heard any sign of the townspeople, they continued on without stopping for close to half an hour.

Just when it seemed the forest was endless, they reached a break in the trees and found themselves standing before an enormous field of tall, untamed grass, the waist-high blades swaying gracefully in the rain and wind. Perhaps two hundred yards away, an old and obviously abandoned barn stood rotting in the middle of the field. Beyond it and the far side of the field was more forest.

With jagged spears of lightning stabbing the ever-darkening sky and thunder throttling the earth, they ran across the field. Into the open. Into the rain. Wading through the grass, their legs grew weaker, their chests burned and they were barely able to breathe. But still, they forced themselves forward until they'd reached the barn.

The building, long deserted, was rotted and littered with numerous wounds in the roof and walls. Rain trickled through the openings, running in constant currents through the cracks and spattering the dirt floor to form small pockets of puddles throughout.

Billy and the others scrambled through an opening where the main door, a large sliding panel, had once stood. It now hung to the side and had nearly broken free of the building altogether. They collapsed to the ground in unison, their labored breath audible above the sounds of the mounting storm, pounding rain and constant trickling and dripping.

After a moment, Billy regained his feet and inspected their surroundings. Although the barn hadn't been used in some time, it retained something of a livestock and manure smell, and remnants of hay and old bags of feed lay scattered about the dirt floor and in the corners of a few dilapidated stalls. He looked next to the high roof, squinting as raindrops splashed his face. Glimpses of the darkening sky shown through the multiple fractures, but otherwise it looked intact and would provide sufficient sanctuary, albeit temporarily. He moved to the remains of the door. Outside, the field they'd crossed was empty. If the townspeople had followed them, they were either hidden in the forest or crawling unseen through the tall grass.

"Are they coming?" Alex asked breathlessly.

Billy ran to the opposite wall, found a hole and checked the hundred or so yards of field in the other direction. It too was empty, the forest beyond it dark and blurred by rain. "I don't see them anywhere, but we can't stay here long, there's no way to defend or secure this place. Too many breaks in the walls and roof, too many ways in, too many directions to keep an eye on. Hurry up and catch your breath."

Stefan pulled his loafers off and rubbed his bare feet. Hardly conducive to running, the shoes had already caused the beginnings of several blisters. "And where, exactly, do you suggest we go?"

"There must be something beyond those woods."

"Right. More woods."

"Sooner or later they've got to come out somewhere."

"I don't care how far we have to go," Alex said, "just so long as we stay ahead of those crazy freaks."

Suddenly, from a dark corner of the barn came a deep but quiet male voice, barely discernable over the relentless rain and occasional thunder.

"They're not crazy," the voice told them. "They're *damned.*"

Chapter Eight

Like victims in a funhouse, they jumped back and scrambled in various directions. Alex let out a muffled scream and skidded to her knees several feet away, backing into a dark corner of her own, while Stefan, leaving his shoes behind, darted toward an opening in one wall of the barn, stopping just shy of squeezing himself through to the outside. Billy had initially backed up a few steps, but now moved forward, closer to the voice, until the shadows parted to reveal its source.

Huddled in the corner, a man watched them from the darkness. About forty or so, his badly receded dark hair was cut short and close to the scalp, which along with his face and neck, was bathed in rainwater that trickled through a gash in the roof above him. His brown eyes were fatigued, his olive skin lined and in need of a shave. He looked as if he'd been sleeping for a very long time, though not particularly well. His hands rested on a sawed-off shotgun lying across his lap, and leaning in the corner over his right shoulder was a machete, its blade glistening and wet. "I won't hurt you," he said, "unless you force me to."

"Who are you?"

The man ran a hand across his head and wiped the water away, but with the continuous flow from above, it was an exercise in futility. He didn't seem to mind. "Name's Eddie Franco."

"The station wagon we saw back in town, was that yours?"

"No." He winced. "It belonged to a family, a young couple with two kids. They got caught here same as you. The townspeople slaughtered them. The rage takes over early on and they don't think clearly until some blood's been shed."

"They killed our friend too," Stefan told him.

"Are you one of them?" Alex asked in a tiny voice.

"Not by choice."

"What does that mean?"

"We need to keep moving," Billy said. "You're safe for now."

"*Safe?*" Alex glared at him, eyes moist. "I won't ever feel *safe* again."

"They won't attack," he said. "Not right away. The rage ends in most of them once there's a few kills. By now they're thinking rationally again, understanding what's at stake. From here it's all about the ritual."

"Which is?" Billy asked.

"Did you find the library in town?"

"Yes. We saw the books on Boxer and Lithobolia."

He bowed his head, better concealing it in shadow.

Stefan stepped closer. "*Please* tell us what's going on. What have we stumbled into?"

"I came here eighteen years ago, summer of '65. My wife and I were on our way up north, got caught in a storm and wound up here. Lauren was her name." He looked to the dirt floor. "They killed her not far from here."

With his silence, only the sound of rain running through fissures in the old barn remained.

"You must've been right around our age back then," Alex said.

"I was the same age I am now. Been sleeping is all. Or whatever it is we do when everything goes dark."

"This guy's a loon." Billy returned to the far wall to check the field. "Still no sign of them out there, let's move."

"There's nowhere to go."

"How can this be?" Stefan asked, a frantic edge returned to his voice. "We tried every possible road and—"

"They all led you right back to Boxer Hills." Franco smiled a little, as if mistakenly. "To understand, you have to know the history. They always lead the trapped to the library, didn't you read the books?"

"We read the basics about Alton Boxer and town history,

and we saw his portrait hanging in the library," Alex explained, doing her best to recall as much as she could from the book. "He was a defrocked minister who came here, established this town with his followers in the 1690s after witnessing strange happenings in a New Hampshire town where stones and rocks fell from the sky. It was blamed on Lithobolia. Boxer claimed he'd seen the entity firsthand, made contact with it and understood the truth of it all, and from then on worshiped him. He preached immortality through submission to sin and—"

"While the Puritans in Salem were hanging so-called witches on the testimony of hysterical little girls," Franco interrupted, "Boxer was controlling everything and everyone in this village through the use of *real* demonic forces, promising immortality and endless hedonistic pleasure. But what he didn't tell the townspeople was that the immortality they were chasing came with a terrible price. There was a catch." Raindrops blinked free of his eyes. "With the Devil there always is."

"I don't believe in the Devil," Stefan said sternly.

"He doesn't care what you believe."

"Satan and eternal damnation, it's all a bedtime story told to children to frighten and intimidate them into behaving themselves. It's religious propaganda and brainwashing, nothing more."

Franco stroked the shotgun. "You have to understand who he really is, what he really is. It's only in later Christian writings that Lucifer's described as falling from Heaven and having a war with God. The early believers described Lucifer as a prosecutor, the angel who made the case against Man when we broke God's laws. Lucifer had no problem with God. It was Man he considered weak and useless for anything other than slaves. Angels were superior beings, why should they bow down before God's newest creation if they weren't worthy of that respect? Lucifer didn't hate God. He hated us."

"What was the catch?" Billy asked. "You said there was a catch."

"Everyone has their time, their day to die. If you don't die, someone else has to. The only way Lithobolia would spare Boxer's soul and the souls of the townspeople, thereby giving them immortality, was if someone else's soul was handed over to him in their place. Someone had to die for them to live. So they began ritualistic murder, incorporating it into their ceremonies and masses to Lithobolia. Outsiders, people passing through, whoever they could get a hold of were slaughtered during their rituals to save themselves." Franco shifted his position a bit, turning toward a grumble of thunder in the distance. "It went on like that for years, until things started to change. The world was changing, modernizing. It got harder to hide who they were and what they were up to. Things were less rural, and when people disappeared, others looked for them. There were fewer victims available, people they could chance killing. And once you run out of food, you eat your own. Newborn children, they were the easiest."

"Good Lord."

"In time," Franco continued, "with the continual slaughter of their offspring, they started to hate themselves. But they hated Boxer even more, and they eventually turned on him too. Late in the summer of 1947, the townspeople killed Boxer in one of his own sick rituals. He was over three hundred years old. They thought killing him would end it all, that it would finally free them, but what they didn't count on was how angry Lithobolia would be. Boxer was his emissary, his gatherer of souls. And those souls, those slaves in the afterlife, they're what make those like Lithobolia so powerful."

"What happened to the town?" Billy asked.

"Lithobolia destroyed it. If you look at the official records, the State of Maine claims Boxer Hills was destroyed by a freak storm in 1947, a horribly violent nor'easter that included torrential rains, hail, hurricane-force winds and even the brief appearance of a tornado. The official records indicate nearly all one hundred and eighty residents were killed. Those who allegedly survived supposedly moved on and the town was never rebuilt. It sits empty now, run down and mostly rotted, only partially standing buildings set back in an overgrown section of forest miles off the state highway. It's a forgotten ghost town, a memory."

"But we're standing in it right now," Alex said.

"The town's cursed. For eighteen years it sleeps, and the souls trapped here sleep right along with it. Not alive, not dead but caught somewhere in between. And then for one day, one span of twenty-four hours, the town of Boxer Hills returns just as it was in 1947 before its destruction. Whoever's caught in town at the time is free game for the souls trapped here. But if they just kill you outright, the way some do when they first come awake filled with the rage, your soul's freed and on its way to wherever it was headed before any of this happened. It's once the ritual begins, the gathering, if they get you then, it's their ticket out. It's their chance for redemption, deliverance. But the Devil doesn't give you anything for free. There are no passes, only trades." He ran his hand along his balding head again, wiping away the rain, pushing it down across his face. "None of the townspeople in Boxer Hills can get to Heaven without sending someone else to Hell."

"What happens after the twenty-four hours?" Alex asked.

"The town vanishes."

"Where does it go?"

"I don't know. All its inhabitants sleep."

"For another eighteen years, and then it reappears and this happens for a single day all over again?"

Franco nodded.

"It's like some sort of demonic Brigadoon, for Christ's sake." Stefan laughed lightly, his hands clutching either side of his head. "You've got to be fucking kidding me."

"That's why the window in the general store moved the way it did," Billy said, "and why everyone was drinking coffee and acting like they'd just woken up. The town had just reappeared. It was still…"

"Becoming," Franco finished for him.

"Why eighteen years?" Alex asked.

"It's the Devil's number. Three sixes equal eighteen."

"What happens if we avoid this ritual, and after twenty-four hours we're still alive?"

"You're free."

"How much longer do we have?"

Franco looked to the cracks in the roof, the rain splashing

across his eyes and forehead. "It's already dark. You get to dawn, you've made it."

"If all this is true," Stefan said, "then why are *you* still alive?"

"They killed my wife. They captured me."

"So this ritual," Billy said, "it was performed on you."

He unfastened the buttons on his shirt and peeled the drenched material away from his skin to reveal a chest covered with a hideous network of scars, the skin stretched tight over an uneven skeletal structure. It looked as if his chest had been crushed then haphazardly reconstructed.

"Then you're one of them," Alex said.

"It's all a lie, don't you get it? No matter how right they think they are, no matter how fanatical their beliefs become, no one gets to Heaven through murder and torture. Their first mistake was trusting Alton Boxer. Their second was in trusting the false god they worship."

"But why are you different from the rest?"

"I'm doomed no matter what I do. I gave my soul to Lithobolia, but they can't force me to play his games. There are only a few renegades among the flock, we don't last too many of these cycles. But none of that matters to me." He closed his shirt. "They may have killed Lauren eighteen years ago, but to me it's only been a day. I know God's still out there somewhere, and she's with Him. Maybe if I do what's right, I can…" He pawed tears from his eyes. "Last time, I just wanted to sleep."

"And now?"

Franco picked up the shotgun and rested the sawed-off barrel against his shoulder. "I want to know that wherever I wake up, it won't be here."

Outside, in the distance, someone screamed, and the sound of a fireball igniting and bursting echoed through the now early evening.

In a single frantic rush, Billy, Alex and Stefan ran to the door they had entered and looked out at the field.

A large bonfire had been set at the edge of the forest. Even through the heavy rain, it burned, its flickering flames providing sufficient light to see the decaying bodies of those who had been killed or come before them. Demonic trophies hanged from trees, dangling like gutted and mutilated rag dolls, Tory among them, the bodies swaying in the mounting wind.

Scattered throughout the forest's edge, the field and around the bonfire, numerous townspeople stood chanting their blasphemous prayers, eerie voices echoing across the field and through the rain, the night.

Mesmerized, Billy and the others watched and listened.

The ritual—the gathering of souls—had begun.

Chapter Nine

The prayers continued like a dirge, the voices droning above the sounds of the storm. In the other direction, the field remained empty, tall blades of grass barely visible through the darkness and rain, moving slowly, back and forth with the wind. Billy watched the night. He'd always looked at things as if he were doing so for the last time, always approached things in his short life with abandon, attacking them head on, as though every day were his last on Earth and his final chance to experience everything being alive entailed. He'd died onstage countless times and in numerous incarnations, but now he felt like he really might be up against his final hours. "Why are they leaving us an escape route?"

"You can't see them in that direction, but they're there." Franco rose to his feet, and holding tight to the shotgun, reached for the machete. Freed from shadows, he looked more formidable. A wide scar ran the length of his right cheek, and the sleeves on his shirt had been torn away to reveal thick, well-muscled arms. An uncontrollable twitch danced across his face and down into his neck. He clenched shut his eyes in an attempt to control the darkness growing within him. When the spasm had passed, he handed Billy the machete.

The cold grip and weight of the large knife filled his hand.

"Your only chance is to make it to those woods on the far side of the field," Franco said, breathing heavily. "If you get that far, follow the forest straight through 'til dawn."

"What'll hit us between here and there?"

"Most are gathered around the fire in prayer. They're conjuring their master." Franco shook his head, as if to dislodge those things slithering through him, changing him, turning him toward the darkness to which his tortured soul was pledged. The prayers of the others seemed to make it worse, but he continued to resist until he was again able to speak. "They'll come in a wave from the direction of the fire and storm the barn. They'll leave others scattered in the field between here and the woods. They're out there, but there'll be fewer of them. Just understand they won't stop. This is their chance to put their souls to rest. They're human, but the deeper into the ritual they go, the more powerful they get, the less human they...we... become. No matter what you do, how many you kill or how far you run, they'll keep coming. They'll try to take you alive. Don't let that happen. When you see the sun rise, that's when you'll know you've made it, not a moment before."

Billy turned to the others. "I'm gonna head straight for them. You two cut out the back, head across the field and make a run for the woods. I'll veer off and lead as many of them away from you as I can."

"Bullshit," Stefan said, hastily pushing his feet back into his loafers. "We're staying together."

"If we stay together we die."

"Then we die together," Alex said firmly.

"No. I'll outrun them and we'll all see each other again come morning." He gave a sad smile as rainwater dripped from his face, the dagger earring swinging in the near dark. "Besides, it's a great part, and you know me, always a sucker for the tragic."

"We don't have to do it like this," Stefan said, eyes moist. "We can—"

"I've always felt pressed for time, you know that. I've always known it was running out on me faster than most. That's why I am the way I am, man. I just never knew why." He handed Stefan the machete. "Now I do."

Wind lashed the barn, spraying through the holes and gashes in the building. And as suddenly as the prayers began, they stopped.

"Stef, get her out," Billy said, eyes burning with intensity. "You hear me? You get her the hell out." He looked to Alex. "Get each other out. This is the only chance we've got."

Alex threw her arms around him, hugging him so tightly he could barely breathe. "Please, Billy," she whispered in his ear. "*Please* don't—"

"Alex, look at me. Who am I?"

She held his face in her hands, the same wild and defiant face she'd never been able to resist. It blurred through her tears. "You're Billy the Kid," she said, laughing and crying at once. "And you can do anything."

"True enough." He gently pushed her toward Stefan, and as she left him, a cold sensation bled through and washed over him, something efficient and deadly and final. With it, there might be some chance of survival. Without it, he—and quite possibly the others—were already dead.

With steely resolve, Alex grabbed a loose board roughly the length of a baseball bat hanging from one of the decaying stalls and tore it free.

"Hurry," Franco warned. "They're coming."

Hand in hand, Stefan and Alex headed for the opening in the far wall. With a final desperate look back, they stepped into the night.

Franco handed Billy the shotgun. "Go ahead, take it."

"What about you?"

He pulled a revolver from the back of his belt. "Good luck."

Billy held his stare a moment, and though no words were spoken, a great many things passed between them.

Something above them cracked and splintered a section of roof, sending small pieces of wood spiraling down with the rain. The horrible stench of sulphur filled the air. "Don't look," Franco warned. "He wants you to look. Don't."

Despite his terror, Billy struggled to remain perfectly still.

Ignoring his own advice, Franco slowly raised his head skyward.

Inhuman yellow eyes pierced the night, peeking down at him through a gash in the wet roof.

Above the clamor of rain, Billy heard the steady flapping of what sounded like large leathery wings.

Franco cocked the hammer on the revolver. "*Go.*"

With a deep breath, Billy ran to darkness.

Behind him, the roof gave way and something descended through the rainy night amidst falling planks and rotted boards.

Franco fired, filling the barn with a deafening blast and a bloodcurdling scream, but neither prevented him from being cast into a relentless darkness of his own.

As Stefan and Alex ran through the field, the rain fell heavy and hard, and the waist-high grass swirled around them as if by magic. The night had become thick as fog, and even at this distance the smell of the bonfire hung in the air.

They had covered half the distance necessary to reach the forest when a shadowy form sprung up out of the grass and lunged for Alex. Stopping to plant her feet and gripping the board with both hands, she let loose a primal scream and swung at it with everything she had. The plank snapped in half across the attacker's chest as the impact reverberated through her wrists, up her arms and into her shoulders. The man grunted and fell, absorbed back into the darkness from which he'd come. Off balance, she stumbled and nearly fell, but Stefan appeared at her side, grabbed hold of her arm and dragged her forward through the night. "Keep moving!" he called above the din of thunder. "We're almost there!"

Lightning tore through the night above them, turning the world an electric blue long enough to illuminate the outline of nearby trees.

Stefan was right; they had nearly reached the forest.

But their glimmer of hope was dashed as several silhouettes emerged from the sea of black before them, slowly rising up through the grass.

They were on him within seconds of moving through the barn doorway, darting out from the darkness, reaching for him and screeching at him like banshees. Billy fired at the first man he saw, blowing him back and away. But another immediately took his place. Without slowing his pace, he braced the butt of the shotgun against his side, pumped, swung it around and fired again. The man wailed as a section of his torso blew apart, and the body tumbled away, swallowed by the grass.

Wind and rain tore at Billy's face, and the untamed grass made his legs feel like they'd been submerged in wet cement. But when he saw a wave of townspeople coming at him from behind the bonfire, shoulder to shoulder and sweeping across the field like a single predatory organism, he veered off as planned and kept running.

Stefan and Alex dove forward through the grass and slid on their bellies, blades tearing at their faces and bodies until they came to a stop in the wet earth.

Rolling to her side, Alex found Stefan's face peering back through the night at her, his expression a mix of disbelief and horror. He brought a trembling finger to his lips, signaling her to be quiet and remain still. She nodded as the rain pounded them, the rich smell of grass and soil filling her nostrils. Pushing her hands through the muddy and loose dirt for purchase, she realized she was still clutching a jagged stump of wood from the broken plank. Somehow, she found comfort in this.

Stefan cocked his head toward his machete, as if this might somehow reassure her, and then cautiously raised his head in an attempt to see through the grass. After a moment, he pointed straight ahead, held up a single finger then pointed to their left and held up three, staring at her to be certain she understood. Though she couldn't be completely sure Stefan could do what was necessary when and if the time came, with a deep sense of vulnerability and helplessness, she gave another nod, and together they crawled forward through the grass.

Run. All he could do was run. Even though he now realized how futile this was. Maybe he'd known all along. It didn't much matter anymore. He'd covered quite a distance but his legs were weak, his chest burned and his body was no longer capable of continuing. Barely able to breathe, Billy forced himself forward until his knees buckled and he crashed to the ground with enough force to separate him from what little air remained in his lungs.

He flopped onto his back, struggling for air. Somewhere above him, lightning blinked, offering a glimpse of the night

sky. Even in tiny flashes it seemed so immense there, so vast
and free.

As they came closer, he heard them rustling the grass,
searching for him. He pumped the shotgun and pulled the
trigger, but there was only an empty click. Raising it like a
club, he somehow managed to regain his feet. As he turned,
thunder cracked and something caught him in the throat. A
warm and sticky wetness spattered his chin and neck. Before
any pain could register, he was down again. Head spinning and
rain splashing his face, he reached for his throat. His hand came
back slick with blood. *Not thunder,* he thought, *not this time. I'm
shot. They shot me.*

The grass parted, and the faces of the damned appeared. So
cold and harsh, such smug assuredness on their pitiless faces,
he thought, and so many of them: children, the elderly, and
everything in between.

He tried to swing the shotgun at them but it flew free of his
grasp, made slippery by rain and blood, and spiraled off into
darkness. Hands came from everywhere, fastening onto him
and pulling him, dragging him back across the field. A flash
of something in the night, perhaps the sole of a boot or heavy
shoe, lurched into his range of vision. It slammed his face and
everything went black.

Anywhere, she thought. *They could come at us from anywhere. They're
all around us.* Continuing to inch forward, carefully parting the
grass as they went, fingers clawing through soft earth, Alex
looked back over her shoulder to make certain nothing was
closing in from behind them. She saw only darkness and slowly
swaying stalks set to a soundtrack of thunder and driving rain.
As she turned back, Stefan reached out with his free hand and
grabbed her wrist, his flesh wet and cold and hard, as if he were
already dead. Their eyes met, and he swallowed so hard she saw
his Adam's apple bounce along his thin throat. Drenched and
dripping, his hair plastered to the sides of his face, he looked
impossibly young, like a child really. But more than the sorrow,
more than the terror, it was the uncertainty that bothered her.
This was a man who carried bugs outside rather than step

on them, a man who had quite possibly never had a physical confrontation in his life.

Stefan broke the spell, turning toward the darkness ahead of them.

She followed his stare, and her stomach clenched.

A man was standing perhaps ten feet from them, his silhouette slightly darker than the night sky stretched out above them. Though darkness obscured his features and the height of the grass only allowed her to see him from the waist up, the outline in his hands clearly indicated he was holding a rifle. The man stood perfectly still, but with a robotic motion, his head slowly panned back and forth as he scanned the field.

When she looked again to Stefan, he had gotten to his knees, the machete in one hand, the large blade glistening in the rain, and the other flat against the ground for balance.

Do it, she thought. *Do it.*

Stefan stared at the man for several seconds, eyes rapidly blinking away rain as his chest rose and fell, the machete shaking horribly.

And just when she thought they might lay hidden in the grass forever, Stefan launched himself forward and to his feet, raising the blade high.

The man's head turned and locked on him.

Stefan froze.

Alex scrambled to her feet as the man swung the rifle around, hitting Stefan in the side of the head with the butt.

As Stefan fell back and the machete flew from his grasp, the man turned toward Alex, but she was already punching the jagged piece of wood at him, driving it up and into this man who towered over her with every ounce of strength she possessed. And it felt as if she'd punched straight through him, puncturing him like a *piñata*.

It wasn't until the momentum had caused her to fall forward and drop to one knee that she realized the man had fired into the air, perhaps reflexively. He staggered back, one hand holding the rifle now and the other pawing desperately at the shard of wood protruding from his bloody windpipe. He fired a second time then fell straight back, disappearing beneath the grass.

Another shadow appeared and headed straight for them.

Stefan regained his feet, retrieved the machete and screamed, "Go!"

Alex ran on, off-balance and awkwardly wading through the grass, the long blades slowing her, trying to trip her and drag her down.

She had just reached the trees when somewhere in the darkness behind her, Stefan cried for help.

The next thing Billy was aware of was agonizing pain. Flat on his back, pinned and unable to move, excruciating crushing pressure had been applied to his chest, abdomen and legs to the extent that he could barely breathe. Frenzied panic set in but only made it more difficult for him to draw air, so he struggled to concentrate on something else—anything—that might help keep him under some semblance of control. Although his vision was blurred with sweat and blood, he was able to make out his captors gathered around and looking down at him with grim faces, lips moving in unison.

"Wilt thou give thyself to him?"

He offered no response, and the crushing pressure in his chest increased. Blood and bile gurgled up into the back of his throat. Until now, terrifying as these hours had been, it all seemed wildly fantastic and not quite real. But this pain, this inability to move left no doubt. This was no dream, no hallucination, no performance laced with Method acting reality.

He was back in the stone church, and he was dying. They were killing him. Slowly.

Alex whirled back around as he called for her again, and she spotted him several yards away, staggering through the grass. Something was on his back. A child. God almighty, it was just a child. A little girl with long blond hair, small arms wrapped around his throat, legs hooked around his waist and her teeth sunk deep into his shoulder.

Stefan still held the machete in one hand, and was trying to reach back and pry her off with the other. But she was clamped on tight.

When she reached him, Alex grabbed the girl's hair and yanked, wresting her small body free. Stefan dropped to his knees as the child was dislodged and fell to the ground several feet away. "It's just a little girl," Alex cried, "a child!"

"Kill it!" Stefan screamed.

The girl was on her feet quickly, feral eyes burning night.

"Stop," Alex said, short of breath and hands out in front of her. "Don't!"

Screaming for the others, the child rushed her, bloody teeth bared.

Stefan staggered between them, and with a single violent swing buried the machete in the side of the girl's neck. With a nauseating *thwack*, it split her to the collarbone. As he let go, leaving the blade buried deep within her, the girl oddly made no sound at all. After another fitful step forward, she pitched into the dark and fell at Alex's feet.

Lightning split the sky.

Stefan grabbed Alex's hand, and together, they slipped into the forest.

With the next wave of pain, Billy's eyes slid shut, and in the back of his mind he saw Jesse staring him down at the theater back on Cape Cod.

We've got the same life waiting for us.

No, he thought. *Not even.*

He thought of his family, how they'd never see him again, and how they'd never know what had happened. Unless Alex and Stefan made it, his death—all their deaths—would forever remain a mystery, relegated to some missing persons file along with countless others. They'd eventually become statistics and little else, a group of young people who got into a car one summer morning on Cape Cod, drove off headed for Maine, and vanished without a trace into thin air.

The chanting brought him back.

"Wilt thou give thyself to him?"

Four men in ceremonial black robes and hoods held a sedan chair, a small windowed cabin atop two long horizontal wooden poles, slowly carrying it up the aisle toward an ancient throne next to the altar. Markings similar to Egyptian hieroglyphics graced the sides of the enclosed structure, and the dark curtains that hung in the windows were drawn to conceal whatever sat inside.

Their god, Billy thought, *carried to its temple.*

From behind the curtains came a low growl.

The chanting grew louder then louder still.

"Wilt thou give thyself to him?"

Behind the curtains the demon sat in judgment, awaiting his decision.

Billy could smell it.

Chapter Ten

The townspeople have assembled in the stone church. Standing in rows and quietly chanting, clad in pilgrim garb from the 1600s—the men in linen shirts, black coats, black felt hats, breech pants to the knees, stockings and leather shoes, and the women in ankle-length petticoats and bodices, their hair up and tucked beneath white bonnets—they remind Alex of actors staging a recreation at a historical site. But she, of all people, knows better.

Nude, and on hands and knees in the aisle leading to the altar, Alex is shackled with heavy chains that cut into her flesh, weigh down her wrists and ankles and make movement difficult. She remembers, struggling as they ripped her clothes away, beat and shackled her. Bathed in blood, some hers, some not, she fights the weight of the chains and her own exhaustion, crawls forward toward the altar, sliding along the filthy floor in small increments.

Before the altar, on a slab of stone, lies Billy. A large wooden board has been placed atop him. It is covered with large rocks. Another pile of stones sits nearby, and two burly men hold a fresh block, ready to add it to the others once given the order.

The church blurs and tilts as Alex fights to retain consciousness.

"You're killing him," she says, or tries to. "You're killing him."

Near the altar stands a skeletal middle-aged man in dark robes. He stares at Billy with his black eyes, a smile pursing his thin lips.

Alton Boxer.

To his left is an ancient throne constructed of bone and human skin.

Alex cannot quite see who or what sits upon it, but something wet and scaled moves and slithers about its base. A tail, she thinks, watching as it slinks between two clawed feet planted firmly on the floor.

God help us.

As her mind fractures, she squints through the haze.

"Wilt thou give thyself to him?"

Billy manages to whisper something and the chanting ceases.

A woman comes forward, leans closer and turns her ear to Billy's mouth in an attempt to better hear him. When he repeats his answer, he does so in a strained and garbled voice, blood from a gunshot wound in his throat gurgling free and dripping to the floor. But his words are unmistakable.

"Fuck you."

His head lolls to the side, and Alex realizes he has seen her.

His expression of defiance turns to sorrow. He holds her gaze, hides there, tunnels into her soul to all the memories they share. Now…and forever.

A reptilian finger resting on the arm of the throne casually points, and the two men place the next stone on the pile.

Something breaks in Billy this time, and his head comes forward violently, as if he's trying to sit up. Blood explodes from his mouth, nostrils and eyes, bursting forth in a spraying mist, and with a final gurgling groan, his body gives way beneath the weight.

As Alex is dragged forward by her chains and deposited before the throne, she looks up into the yellow eyes glaring at her from the unbearable face of Lithobolia, and knows she's next.

"Billy's dead."

Her eyes opened and the nightmare receded, returning her to the forest.

Stefan sat nearby, beneath a large tree. Soiled with blood and soaked from the rain, he stared at the ground with a despair she had never before seen in him. "We don't know that," he said softly.

They had spent most of the night walking or running, constantly on the move, and when they hadn't encountered anyone in hours and grew weary with exhaustion, they'd finally stopped beneath a cluster of trees. Alex remembered sitting and leaning against a tree, allowing her eyes to close for what she thought would just be a moment or two. But from the look of the ash-colored sky, she'd been asleep awhile longer than that.

"He's dead," she said again.

Stefan seemed too destroyed emotionally to argue. "Plans," he said, absently rubbing his wounded shoulder. "All those plans we had, we..."

Alex got to her feet. The forest was quiet and still dripping with moisture, but the storm had passed and taken the rain with it. Every muscle in her body ached. "We better get going."

"I killed a child," he said, voice cracking. "I killed a...*child*, I..."

"We need to keep moving until morning, just like Franco said."

"It's nearly dawn." Stefan sighed. "Look."

In the distance, through the trees, the sun was slowly peeking over the horizon, turning the far sky an ethereal blend of orange and red. She watched it awhile then looked around, trying to gain some sense of bearing, but the forest was vast and thick, and the light had not quite reached them yet.

"We've made it," he said wearily.

She didn't know whether to laugh or cry. They'd done it, they were free.

A cracking sound echoed through the forest.

When you see the sun rise, that's when you know you've made it.

Alex whirled about, and as more sounds of snapping twigs and restless movement shattered the silence, she looked skyward.

Not a moment before.

The treetops were just visible against the sparse beginnings of daylight.

"They're above us," she heard herself say.

They're human, but the deeper into ritual they go...

The forest exploded into deafening cracks as tree branches split and snapped in one sudden wave, sounding as if the woods themselves were collapsing, coming down around them.

...the more powerful they get...the less human they become...

And from the trees came blurs—dark forms in period clothing—dropping from the sky, smashing tree limbs as they went, groans and growls mixed with the thudding impact as they hit the ground, falling all about them.

With a horrific scream, Alex was gone, snatched away and dragged back through the woods.

As the others crept closer, Stefan bowed his head and began to weep.

A gentle breeze drifted through the open bedroom windows, the white lace curtains fluttering, billowing deeper into the room then returning to rest as the wind chimes outside again came to life. Their delicate song should have relaxed her, but she was still too close to the nightmares. She remembered the horrible smell that filled her nostrils while yellow, fiery eyes gawked down at her, gliding roughly back and forth above her as the beast they belonged to slammed into her with boundless violence and depravity. She remembered being chained in that awful church, her breasts and stomach and thighs slick with blood as he demanded allegiance.

Wilt thou give thyself to him?

Old nightmares, she told herself, *bad dreams.*

The horrific memories retreated, and she felt warmth coming from the body next to her, wafting from his nude flesh to hers. Rolling from bed, she padded across the bedroom to a rocking chair in the corner. Her clothes lay across the seat. She stepped into a pair of panties then pulled on a bra.

"Is it morning?" Stefan asked, his speech still slurred from sleep.

"Yes."

"I remember," he told her.

She looked at him quizzically.

"You said I was crying in my sleep…weeping." Stefan swung his feet around to the floor, sat up and rubbed his eyes. "I remember."

"It woke me." She put her sweatshirt on, dropping it down over her head and letting it fall loosely into place as she stepped in front of the free-standing antique mirror against the wall. She froze a moment, and then carefully fluffed her hair, spiking it with her fingers as best she could. "I was dreaming of the forest. In the dream we didn't make it. They came out of the trees and got us."

He remained on the edge of the bed, head in his hands. "I'm so...*angry*."

Neither suspected they'd one day end up together, existing in this lonely old house with their memories and nightmares of that awful summer day. But here they were. "1983 was a long time ago, Stef. It's 2001."

"I'm almost forty years old," he said.

Alex slipped her jeans on then slid the curtains open on the window facing the street. The sun had almost fully risen, ushering in a beautiful new day.

But beauty, as they had come to learn, really was only skin deep.

"We're immortal," she told him, the mantra swirling through her head.

"But there's a catch."

"With the Devil there always is."

"No passes, only trades."

"One day. This day."

Through the window, Alex saw the townspeople gathered outside near the street. They watched the house with impassive faces, ready to welcome the new members of their brood to the fold.

"They're waiting for us," she said.

Tracing the scars across his chest with his fingertip, Stefan nodded woefully and began to dress.

For a moment, Alex had allowed herself to forget. When she first came awake, she'd thought perhaps they really had made it out all those years ago, survived that hellish day and gone on to have a life together elsewhere, relegating all else to the realm of memory and shadow. But she knew the truth. They both did.

There could be no deliverance in the past, only in the certain carnage of the future. Their salvation, their very souls, depended on it.

And the clock was ticking.

Author's Note

*C*atching Hell is, of course, entirely a work of fiction. It was, however, very loosely inspired by true events experienced by myself and others one summer in the early 1980s. Though the characters, several locations and many major plot points have been changed, altered or completely fictionalized, in reality, on that strange summer day so many years ago, those of us who were involved found ourselves in a bizarre New England town and unwittingly swept into a terrifying situation that in many ways remains as much of an enigma now as it was then. Though we weren't looking for trouble, we were young, often reckless, and in our own ways, chasing a little hell. What we hadn't banked on was actually catching it. See you on the road.

—Greg F. Gifune
Friday, April 13th, 2007
New England. Night.

About the Author

Greg F. Gifune is a professional, best-selling, internationally-published author of several acclaimed novels, novellas and two short story collections. Working predominantly in the horror and crime genres, Greg has been called, "The best writer of horror and thrillers at work today" by New York Times best-selling author Christopher Rice, "One of the best writers of his generation" by both *The Roswell Literary Review* and horror grandmaster Brian Keene, and "Among the finest dark suspense writers of our time" by legendary best-selling author Ed Gorman. Greg's work has been published all over the world, translated into several languages, received starred reviews from *Publishers Weekly, Library Journal* and others, is consistently praised by readers and critics alike, and has garnered attention from Hollywood. His novel THE BLEEDING SEASON, originally published in 2003, has been hailed as a classic in the horror genre and is considered to be one of the best horror/thriller novels of the decade. Greg resides in Massachusetts with his wife Carol, a few cats and two dogs, Dozer and Dudley. He can be reached online at gfgauthor@verizon.net or on Facebook and Twitter. Visit his official site for updates and info at:

https://gregfgifune.wordpress.com/

Curious about other Crossroad Press books?
Stop by our site:
http://store.crossroadpress.com
We offer quality writing
in digital, audio, and print formats.

www.ingramcontent.com/pod-product-compliance
Lightning Source LLC
Chambersburg PA
CBHW030538180626
46810CB00005B/1926